YOU, ME, HIM, AND HER

BY

MARCUS CARTER

To Lynn
My favorite lil' firecracker
I always look forward to our pow-wows
They made this book
MC

Copyright © 2011 by Marcus Carter
All rights reserved. This book or any portion thereof
may not be reproduced or used in any manner whatsoever
without the express written permission of the author
except for the use of brief quotations in a book review.
Printed in the United States of America

First Printing, 2011

PROLOGUE

"I'm going to ask you a question, and I want you to be honest with me."

Neko Rose looked at his girlfriend Chloe Bryant as if she had just asked him if he believed in God. The two self proclaimed soul mates, who both acknowledged that men are from Mars and women are from Venus, were looking at each other as if that distance wasn't a few planets but a few galaxies. The two twenty-six year olds, together for over two and half years now, had already graduated to that point where they could easily communicate without speaking. Neko desperately wished the two could put that skill to use right now. Neko, who at this point was only 25% engaged in the conversation was not a professional, but was starting to understand the rules of the game. So even as he scanned last night's NBA scores on his new iPhone Chloe had gotten him for his birthday, he made sure to look up with a mask of concern and understanding after every sentence Chloe uttered. He had tried tirelessly to reassure Chloe that there was nothing the young couple couldn't conquer if they only communicated, but was overwhelmed at times by how often Chloe wanted to put this theory to the test. *"I've created a monster,"* he thought to himself while his mouth spit out the words, "of course, baby."

Neko was dead tired, and coming down from the boost that the 5 Hour Energy he had taken had given him. While impressed with the initial results, he was wondering if he was falling prey to Chloe's banter or false advertising, because he was ready to nod off. Just fall asleep right in the middle of what he saw shaping up as one of Chloe's classic conversations after only taking the energy boost two hours ago. And for a second he mentally went back to that point in the gas station this morning where he stood in front of the counter contemplating if he could mix Red Bull with a 5 Hour Energy. He knew he was taking the morning to accompany Chloe even after an all-nighter at work. At his moment of truth he decided against it, opting simply for the 5 Hour Energy. Neko hoped that the mornings errands would run smoothly and he'd be in bed by noon. He didn't want to risk that for anything, so even pissing Chloe off by being short with her wasn't an option, he just hoped she would take it easy on him. Although he assumes that Chloe will not make him endure her psychobabble, he is fully aware that if she decides to take it there, he's going, no questions asked. Back in reality, Neko knows Chloe too well. Like how she sets up her line of questions with a line of questions. There is definitely always something down the rabbit hole but with Chloe the question is always *how deep the rabbit hole is?*

"I know we've been on and off at times during our relationship, sometimes things were my fault. I promise you I won't get mad so don't worry. But I wanted to know if you had been with anybody besides me?"

Here we go, thought Neko, *here we go.* While Neko is fully aware that all Chloe wants is the truth, be it right or wrong, he also understands that there is in fact a right or wrong answer to her romantic query. He chuckles, as he thinks back to an earlier version of himself who would have had no idea how to answer this question, this very, very loaded question that women always ask as if they really want to know the answer. He mentally checks his *'oh you must think I'm stupid* handbook, cross referencing her question with all available literature on the subject before settling on the best available answer, regardless of truthfulness.

"No baby, nobody."

He answers quickly and confidently, making certain to make and hold eye contact to highlight the desired effect. The ensuing stare down is classic, real Cold War propaganda-ish, but Neko is not shaken. He's seen this movie before and knows exactly how it ends, first one to blink loses. Chloe's no slouch at this either, she knows exactly what she wants to see and hear, *regardless of truthfulness*. Satisfied that Neko has if not passed her test, at the very least exerted a considerable amount of effort, which is all she was looking for anyways. See in Chloe's eyes, she's long stopped looking for the 'perfect' man, content now to be happy with just *her* man. She smiles as Neko simultaneously breathes a silent sigh of relief. Neko knows he has again navigated his way through the jungle which is Chloe's emotional pendulum of bi-polar mental activity. Holding true to his cardinal rule when dealing with her, *remain calm*. But conceding the battle and not the war, Chloe quickly snaps.

"Let me find out you was out there fucking around."

Chloe's tone was half joking, half serious, leaving you to believe she's only joking until it gets serious. Neko, up to task, flashes his game face that gets Chloe every time. He is human, so sometimes these exchanges are nothing more than Chloe making him feel wanted in their own little way, although he is fully aware that her last statement was most definitely a threat.

The young lovers understand the odds. They understand the decadence of the world they live in. So these impromptu Kodak moments are always given their proper due. They smile, as they both replay their own sacrifices made for the other. The energy between the two undeniable, the passion apparent, and the smile on their faces was an illustration.

"Ms. Bryant and Mr. Rose, the doctor will see you now," the nurse interrupts. Chloe and Neko are grabbed by gravity and given instructions to land, but their favorite song is still playing in their minds. They proceed into the doctor's office, walking to their own beat.

I

To say that Chloe was prepared for the information given to her and Neko by Dr. Sharpley would be complete and utter bullshit. Chloe was pregnant, again. As her and Neko strode out of the doctor's office, she was trying her best to keep her nerves in check. The doctor had told her that she was six weeks, which equated to instant weight on her shoulders, as Chloe had psyched herself into believing she wasn't pregnant. She was unsure if Neko had been paying attention or if he was just playing dumb. This situation was a double sided sword. No matter how you sliced it, this was a classic case of the pot calling the kettle black. She and Neko had agreed not to ask questions they really didn't want to know the answers to. She still wondered if Neko had messed around on her. Although her emotions sometimes took her there, she never drove too hard on Neko regarding this subject, fully aware of the skeletons in her own closet. She knew investigating this subject could get ugly, so she decided to back off, acknowledging her guilt. She was dying to know if Neko had stepped out on her, let alone sleeping with some skank unprotected. This was not beyond him at all. Their 29 month relationship was not only a testament to love, but more precisely survival. The young couple had given each other just about every conceivable reason to walk away.

The fact that her and Neko had actually ever even hooked up at all, to this day, still in her head only added up to the flip of a coin. She remembered vividly, chuckling as the thoroughly intoxicated Neko, through slurred speech and all, did everything in his power to convince her to give him her number. His looks didn't hurt. He stood about six feet. He had a caramel complexion, nice build, and seductive brown eyes. Although she wasn't overly curious to what he looked like under his Sean John cardigan with the white V neck underneath, she definitely wanted to know what he could do with those succulent lips he had. Chloe didn't mess around too much, aware that word travels fast, but she wasn't a nun either. Where other drunk overtures in the local pub she ignored because of the opposite sexes over aggressiveness, it was something about Neko's advances she found to be cute. She couldn't put her finger on it, but he made her laugh. Didn't hurt that he kept the champagne flowing and exhibited a confidence that wasn't overbearing but definitely gave off an *'I'm somebody you should* know type of vibe. Even though Neko was a bit past *full,* he still had a vocabulary that extended past "hey shorty, what it do?" This hint of education, combined with his clean good looks, and his ability to have a good time was refreshing. Although she wasn't quite ready to jump in the bed at that point, she had agreed to see Neko again, instructing herself, "If dude got problems, he'll simply kill his own chances." Chloe had heard just about every pick up line and had been on her fair share of dates. She knew without the help of the liquid courage or a crew across the club, most brothers could barely run a conversation. So if Neko wanted to see her *soooo* badly, she reasoned there was nothing wrong with a casual night out, on him of course. Plus, the comedy that was a brother trying to talk up on some ass sometimes was better than Katt Williams standup.

Although Dr. Sharpley had just dropped a bomb, these thoughts still made her smile. As she stepped into the passenger side of Neko's Nissan truck, she looked over at him, continuing to smile, fully aware that with every reason he'd given her to go, he'd given her every reason to stay as well.

II

As Neko navigated away from the doctor's office, en route to his apartment, he stole a glance at Chloe. This wasn't the first, or the second, time Chloe had come up pregnant. And even after the two examples, he still had no idea what to say to her. He had no idea how to say what he really thought and have her understand. Although it made perfect sense to him, he knew no woman wanted to hear her man say, "I'm cool if we have it….and I'm cool if we don't." Neko had no clue what was wrong with that thought process. Neko had learned that if you're curious to how a woman's going to react to something, just give it a minute. Neko wasn't going to over react to the situation, and had decided to go the route of sheer and utter ignorance. Women hate when men resort to this method of dealing with adversity, but to men it's natural.

Neko wasn't a choir boy, but he loved Chloe. Like most males, he blocked out his indiscretions, chalking it up to the *'sorting of his royal oat*. Chloe had skills. Neko sometimes thought she had stepped out on him before, he suspected, but she had a way of squeezing that muscle down there, leaving him relatively brainless as she whispered *'its yours* in his ear. This, along with his own guilt, was usually all the convincing he needed. Besides, if she was on bullshit, *'good luck*, he thought, given she was now pregnant with his seed. Neko, unfortunately, did think this way. He was intelligent, if not diabolical. He had insecurities that existed of course. Chloe Bryant fell into Neko's category of *'if she ain't a dime, she's damn sure a nine*. She was tall, a couple inches short of six feet. She had some weight, but it was in all the right places. She was beautiful, but more Sanaa Lathun than Halle Berry. Although she always took it the wrong way, Neko insisted it was a compliment when he told her she looked just as good with absolutely no makeup on as she did all did up.

Neko maintained his security with a balance that maybe only he understood. He knew of no man that would pass on Chloe if given the chance, but he slept well at night knowing that he loved that girl more than any man ever could. All this was a reflection on how he felt he was the only one who recognized Chloe's true beauty. You could take her to meet your mom, or your boss, and then relax with a six pack, a sack and a ball game. She was a sophisticated, around the way girl. She could grace an elegant evening gown and be confused with beauty queen, then turn and create the same sentiment in jeans and a t-shirt. Neko frowned, knowing that expecting sex when they got back to his apartment might be out of the question, but he was going to shoot his shot. Neko's mere thoughts of Chloe were doing *the usual*, that being putting his dick on rock hard.

Chloe was more excited than Neko that he was able to fall asleep instantly after they reached his apartment. This gave Chloe the opportunity to do what she was dying to do as they left Dr. Sharpley's, call her girls. It was eleven o'clock on a Saturday morning and Chloe could care less about waking up her best friends Tanya and Jazmine. The three women had been friends since the sixth grade, and although neither was thrilled with the weekend wake-up, they would have thrown more of a fuss if Chloe had not called. By 11:03 in the A.M. they were in full swing.

"So what that nigga have to say," questioned Jazmine.

Pessimism had always been her strong suit. The only thing that Jazmine was optimistic about was her assumption that things could most definitely get worse, no matter what the subject was.

"Jazmine, I think we need to be a little bit more constructive right now," Tanya insisted.

Tanya was Jazmines's polar opposite, to her there was always a bright side. Tanya was the type that would have instructed Tina Turner to give Ike another shot. Like clockwork, in a few minutes time, Chloe's issues had also become her two best friends and quite honestly, that's just how they rolled.

"See what you need to do is say 'fuck that nigga, cuz he ain't been nothing but more and more baggage since you met his ass. What ya'll gone raise a family in his teeny-weeny apartment? Load the kid into his old ass Nissan Pathfinder? Chloe get serious; get out while you young, girl please." Jazmine would never be accused of being subtle.

"Chloe you can't do anything rash at this point," countered Tanya. "You can't take the health of your mind, body, and soul so lightly. Getting an abortion should never be an immediate response to the wonderful news that you are preparing to bring a life into this world."

"Cut the 'we are the world bullshit Tanya," Jazmine argued, if these two were ready to have a baby we would be aunties by now."

"But it didn't happen that way Jazmine," snapped Tanya. Tanya was one to look on the bright side, but definitely a 'don't let the smooth taste fool you, as well. "If getting an abortion was the answer to everything, none of us might be here."

"But I bet this nigga ain't spoke one word about keeping this baby, has he Chloe?"

Jazmine spoke matter-of-factly. This back and forth between Tanya and Jazmine was actually how Chloe sorted a lot of her issues out. The yin and yang nature of her friends allowed her to hear both sides, helping her make up her mind. After an hour though, Chloe had no idea what to do, but she had realized something very important, her and Neko hadn't really said a word regarding their current predicament.

IV

Neko awoke to his phone going off about 5:30 that evening. It was a text that read, *Can I see you tonight?* When he felt Chloe lying next to him, he quickly turned to insure she couldn't see it. He knew who it was from, but noticing Chloe roll over, he gave off body language like it was a wrong number or something. Little did Neko know that when men play dumb a little alarm goes off in woman's mind.

"Who was that?"

As Chloe's question rolled off her tongue, Neko, as if on cue, responded.

"Oh, that was smoke, wanted to know if I was hitting the studio tonight."

Smoke was the closest thing to a best friend Neko had. Neko had been making beats since he was 15. He had parlayed his job as an overnight producer at local Chicago radio station Power 92 into a legitimate front to make money from the beats that he worked tirelessly on. Neko was very realistic and understood retiring as a producer comfortably was as likely as hitting the lottery, but it was definitely a passion. If Chloe had any competition for Neko's time, it wasn't with a woman; it was with an MPC beat machine. So when Neko responded the text was from Smoke, Chloe simply groaned, fully aware what this might mean for her chances of talking with Neko that night about how he felt about the news they'd received earlier that day. Neko knew that Chloe disapproved of the time Neko put into his music, so this was a safe cover to direct attention away from the text he received, which at this point he was unsure if Chloe had seen.

"So are you?"

"Am I what?"

"Don't play dumb Neko; are you really thinking about going to the studio tonight, after what happened today?"

Neko knew exactly what she was talking about, but sometimes Neko thought if you avoided certain subjects that they would simply go away. But not this one, he knew Chloe was confused as he was, but wouldn't rest until she got an idea of where his head was at with everything. He was surprised she had actually let him get some sleep. He actually had no studio time booked, but he wasn't sure if he might just want to relax that night, without Chloe.

"I'm not sure, I think Smoke might have somebody that wants to grab a few beats from me."

Smoke was a pretty well-known artist on the Chicago hip hop scene. The two had worked it out where Neko gave Smoke free beats for every beat Smoke helped Neko sell. Whatever distaste Chloe had for Neko's musical endeavors, she never got in the way of Neko making some extra money. Chloe simply sighed. One of those long drawn out sighs that said subliminally, "whatever." Trying desperately to change the subject, Neko tried talking a language they both understood.

"You hungry?"

V

"She text you at the crib? While she know you with Chloe? You must be giving her some of that bionic dick. Some of that Pookie from New Jack City 'I gotta have it, it be calling me dick." Smoke mimicked Chris Rock's memorable lines, "It be calling me." Smoke was having a field day with Neko's personal life. He always did.

"It ain't funny Smoke."

Neko said this as he giggled himself. Neko was like every other man who openly enjoyed talking about women wanting him; it's a guy thing he supposed. Neko was talking to Smoke via Bluetooth as he headed to Harold's Chicken to get food for him and Chloe. Although he didn't discuss his issues in detail with Smoke the way Chloe did with her friends, Neko generally opened up to Smoke simply because he felt like he had to tell somebody. Neko didn't understand why Chloe always consulted Jazmine and Tanya on everything. He was of the general consensus that the more people who know your business, the more you were opening yourself up to ridicule and criticism from people who didn't care that much for you in the first place. Neko placed no stock in people's opinions about his personal life; he was only talking to Smoke right now to stroke his own ego.

"I don't even know if Chloe gone let me talk my way out of the house tonight, plus I don't know if I feeling like fucking with 'ol girl tonight anyway."

Neko spoke as if stepping out to have casual sex was such a huge strain on him. He was posturing now, his secret sex partner was supposed to be a one-time thing that had turned into something more with the help of Remy Martin and Coca Cola.

Neko had no interest in any woman but Chloe, but at 26, monogamy was borderline socially unacceptable. He thought to himself, 'what would people at his age actually have to talk about if not for casual encounters of the cheating kind?'

He tried to picture he and Smoke having a talk where he explained how Chloe was the only woman for him, he then imagined the tear rolling down Smoke's cheek as he whispered, "say it ain't so." This thought caused Neko to chuckle. He had no idea why society frowned upon serious relationships, as he tried to count how many people he knew whose mother and father were still together. It was as if the world was filled with nothing more than baby daddies and baby mommas.

VI

"I'm tied up in the studio all night," Neko texted back to his "dip," as he was walking into his apartment, Fresh from picking up food for him and Chloe. He had made up his mind that he and Chloe needed to talk, but he was hoping to simply support Chloe on whatever she wanted to do. He loved Chloe and had no ideas on planning a future without her. He was prepared to make whatever adjustments he had to make as long as she remained in his life. He would even give up music if he had to. Neko often surprised himself with the lengths he would go to satisfy Chloe. He worried more about making sure he had the means to keep her happy. Chloe had never made money an issue in their relationship, but Neko was no fool. He knew that Chloe enjoyed the treatment that received at restaurants, clubs, and events, all rooted in the connections Neko's job afforded. Neko was privileged to "star" treatment and knew the "right people" all over Chicago. The two hadn't paid for entry to a club or bought a drink in a club in over a year. Chloe always told him how good it made her feel when she could walk to the front of most lines, ahead of other women, as promoters escorted her explaining, "oh, this Neko girl."

Would Chloe go for the straight life? Would she strip him of everything that made Neko Neko, only to lose interest once he gave in to the responsibilities of being the head of a household?" What if after Neko gave this girl what she wanted, she got bored?

Neko truly believed he and Chloe were soul mates. They were notorious for their inside jokes and their ability to simply entertain one another.

But Neko secretly wondered if she was would still look at him the same if the perks of being with Neko Rose ceased to exist?

Neko suddenly realized he was intent on making Chloe happy but had no clue on exactly what made Chloe happy. Neko was very secure and confident in whom he was but at times struggled with if "who he was" could satisfy Chloe. He was afraid of losing her to some chump with big pockets. He had big dreams for him and Chloe and whoever else they brought along with them.

At this point he noticed he was having this moment in the stairwell leading to his apartment. He could smell the odor of marijuana from his neighbor's door. He remembered how nervous his neighbor got about people standing in the hallways because his neighbor sold weed and was super paranoid about the police. Neko realized he did look kind of silly just standing in the hallway and proceeded into his apartment, deadest on talking things out with Chloe.

VII

"Do you want to come by and talk? You know I'm here if you need me."

Chloe was on the phone with her ex-boyfriend Garrett. The two had been broken up for over four years, but kept in touch especially when Chloe was having a tough time. Garrett was also four years Chloe's senior. He had been her first and although they didn't work out, she still always confided in him and from time to time shared other things with him as well. They had a firm grip on exactly what they were doing, and although both were currently in serious relationships, they maintained what the two liked to call an "understanding."

"No Garrett, that's alright. Thanks for taking a few minutes away from wifey to talk to an old friend."

"No problem. Anytime. We got years in the game; you know how I feel about loyalty. That comes before just about anything in my book."

Chloe hung on Garrett's every word. Garrett was a soothing presence in Chloe's life. She appreciated how at the drop of a dime, he could revert back to old times and make her feel like she was the only girl in the world. Garrett had set the standard with her on what she thought a man should be. Over the years she had even forgotten about the cheating when they had been together. She valued what she and Garrett had and although Neko was her man, Garrett wasn't going anywhere.

Neko wasn't necessarily the jealous type, he was aware of the type of attention Chloe received. And although he had a few thoughts swimming in the back of his head, he trusted Chloe. She had earned it in his book. He felt he was just a boy when the two had met and she stuck by him as he went through the growing pains of becoming a man. In a sense, Chloe had molded him like a piece of clay. She was smart enough not to over-react to everything, knowing that this would do nothing more than push him away. She let him figure stuff out on his own, and just stood by his side. She made him feel like a man, and over time he started to act like one. Neko was aware of this and Chloe's patience with him made him love her that much more. Little did he know he was being molded in Garrett's image.

"I love him, Garrett, with all my heart, I really do. But sometimes I do find myself wishing I could talk to him the same way I talk to you, is that wrong?"

Chloe confided in Garrett, her prototype of what a man was. Chloe couldn't imagine how upset Neko would be if he could hear her finding consul in another man. Right now she didn't care; Garrett was giving her what she needed.

"He just doesn't act like he can see more than one day in front...."

Chloe stopped in the middle of her sentence as she opened the bathroom door. And looking her right in the face was Neko. She jumped, but was more startled mentally than physically. How long had he been standing there? What had he heard?

VIII

Get a grip Chloe. Chloe stood in the threshold of Neko's bathroom door trying to catch her bearings. Then she thought to herself, "Straighten up sister before you start to look guilty."

"Ok Jaz, just do what you gotta do girl, a nigga gone do what he gone do anyway. Anyway, Neko just walked in with some Harold's girl, and I am starving, plus you know I'm eating for two now," Chloe mused, "I'll talk to you later, and thanks again for the talk."

Chloe walked past Neko, said "I'm hungry," and mentally crossed her fingers that he hadn't heard anything and was buying her little act. She knew Garrett would understand, and if he didn't, she would have to explain later. Neko was just standing there, and she was about to start explaining when Neko blurted, "Who Jazmine tricked into fucking with her now?" Neko and Jazmine got along in no way, shape, form, or fashion. The two could barely be in the same room together, and the two cracked on each other every chance they got. Chloe knew the only way that they maintained peace between the two was there love for her.

"I don't think you know him, and stop talking bout my friend Neko."

She was slowly relaxing, breathing a sigh of relief as she plopped down on the couch.

"It ain't my fault Chloe that the closest thing Jazmine had to a man all her life was the doctor that cut the cord when she was born. Face it baby, you know it and I know it, the girl can't keep a man because she don't know what to do with that stankin' ass attitude of hers." Neko continued on his rant, "If she would stop comparing every relationship she got in to a Tyler Perry movie, she might just trick some lame into sticking around for a while."

Chloe didn't know Neko cared so much, but was more than happy to be having this conversation than the one they could be having right now.

"Leave her alone Neko," Chloe said between giggles, "the girl just know what she want that's all."

Actually, Chloe thought this was progress. Usually Neko acted as if Jazmine was repulsive, now he was giving dating advice. Maybe he was coming around. It would be such a huge relief if she could have her man and one of her best friends in the room without having to be a referee as the two went at it. Maybe Neko was maturing. She was completely at ease, and for the first time all day, she was hit with a sense of "everything is going to be OK." Neko grabbed what they needed to eat, and plopped down on the couch next to her. The two were about to head off to that place they go Chloe thought. That place where only she and Neko were invited. A nice night, where the drama got checked at the door. All aboard to La La Land.

IX

It was warm. Pleasing to the senses. The aroma was of an inspired casual encounter. It felt like a slight drizzle on a 100 degree day. It looked like a rainbow and it sounded like Trey Songz when he got her to make love faces. La La Land. Neko and Chloe had created this place out of habit. It was there Fortress of Solitude. It was the remix to Lauryn Hill and D'Angelo's classic "Nothing Even Matters." It required no outside stimuli. No phones, no TV, no music, no nothing. The two could quite literally look into one another's eyes and absorb each other's energy, creating a bridge to one another. It gave their eyes a particular rhythm and their minds did a waltz. They would look at each other and smile. A touch could tickle. It was sex without touching. Mental masturbation. A feeling. They couldn't describe it. They tried.

"Close your eyes," Neko instructed, "Give me your hand."

Chloe obliged and extended her hand. He slowly caressed the inside of her palm. She was wide open as a result of his touch. Similar to how it feels when the hairs on the back of your neck stand up or if you were to moisten your skin with a wet kiss then blow on it. As Neko massaged, he whispered into her ear moving close enough that his language was giving her ears head. He held her hand like it was a winning lottery ticket and spoke like he was telling a nation of slaves they are free.

"What am I doing to you Chloe?"

Neko spoke and Chloe was 'in it. Her middle pocket was becoming lubricated around the rim. She was starting to remember things. The images flashing in and out of her head, her nipples standing at attention.

"You're touching me," she confessed.

Neko might as well have been down on one knee. Chloe could imagine all the things Neko could do for her while down on one knee, and every one of them she could think of was good.

Right on point. Neko felt power when he pleased Chloe. Not an authoritative power, but how a father would feel lighting the candles of his daughter's birthday cake. Her happiness was in his hands. He treasured this moment, he lived for this moment. This woman's ecstasy was his drug. He was strung out on her orgasm.

"How do you know I'm touching you," he asked.

He wanted his reward. He wanted his climax. He felt he had earned it. The future didn't matter; the past had only served as a vehicle that had gotten them there. The present was just that, a gift. They were each other's gift and they were thankful.

"I can feel it," Chloe confessed.

This exchange had not been physical. They're minds came. Neither one of them smoked, but they needed a cigarette. La La Land. The softest place on Earth. Where the landscape was a wonderful dream. The "fucking Catalina wine mixer" of the senses. Willy Wonka and the Chocolate Factory with sex drive. They created this place and didn't allow anyone to disrupt them while they were there. It was their Great Escape, their Pina Colada. They came and went as they pleased and all it took to travel was for his eyes to catch hers and a smile.

X

The credits rolled on the movie Chloe and Neko had just watched. While out grabbing food, Neko had decided to make it a Redbox night. As they sat curled up on the couch, Neko checked the nights NBA scores. Chloe smiled and reveled in another of her subtle victories she was starting to get more often. Neko was a sports nut. He rarely missed a game, and could go on for hours when the subject turned to basketball. But Chloe had changed all that. Chloe had inched further up on his things to do list. Earlier in their relationship, Chloe could command Neko's attention before a game or after a game, but now, Chloe could command Neko's attention instead of the game. So even though she could care less, her facial expression was one of jubilation. To Chloe it was the little things that counted. She realized she hadn't felt this good since she had done the impossible and gotten Neko to run to the store for sanitary napkins. First those, now sports. Chloe was infiltrating.

Her victory was short-lived though. After Neko had discovered the Bulls had lost, he didn't bother to watch anymore and casually skimmed through the channels. He stopped at a random reality show. Never one for the senseless drama, Neko had actually developed a tolerance for them because of Chloe. As usual, today's selection, title to remain nameless, depicted either immediate family members or complete strangers about two seconds from strangling each other.

"Fuck you bitch," snapped one luck contestant.

"No, fuck you bitch. Who you calling a bitch, bitch," responded another.

"I call'em how I see'm bitch. And right now I'm looking at a bitch, bitch."

This stuff was priceless. Chloe was entranced as Neko was counting. It amazed him how baseless this was. How many times could two women call each other a bitch in a six minute segment?

"Yeah, you looking at a bitch, bitch! A bad bitch that would whoop another bitch's ass!"

The other young lady, quick to respond, but definitely lacking skill points, "Whoop my ass bitch, come on bitch."

Neko was at double digits and to starting to lose count. Fortunately, the reality show went to commercial. After watching the movie, the clip of the reality show, did just that for Chloe, brought her back to reality. She looked over at Neko, who was again analyzing the TV Guide, trying to figure out something to watch. All the issues of the day came crashing back for Chloe. The doctor visit, the good/bad news about the pregnancy. Her talk with Garrett. It was instantly overwhelming and it was written all over her face. Neko looked over and in a classic example of "men just don't get it," casually blurted out, "I know baby, I know."

At this response, Chloe was presently surprised. She suddenly didn't feel so alone. She felt like finally Neko was taking things seriously. She was proud; all it had taken was time and patience. If she could she would have pat herself on the back for being such a great judge of character, she had always known that Neko was capable of joining her in the real world where they could discuss their issues like adults.

Then reality set in as Neko's face began to match her look of concern.

"I know baby, I should have gotten two Redbox movies," Neko muttered.

Complete and utter buzz kill, Chloe thought. She sighed, knowing that she had quite possibly given Neko too much credit; he was after all, just a man. She quickly gathered her thoughts, wrapping her mind around the idea that she indeed would likely have to beat a conversation out of Neko. Unfortunately for Neko, she was more than prepared to do this if she had to.

"We need to talk Neko," Chloe said sternly.

On cue, Neko switched the TV off, tossed the remote on the coffee table, turned to her with a look of seriousness to match her own and said, "I know."

XI

"Neko we've been together almost three years and I love you very, very much," Chloe started.

Neko listened intently but couldn't help feeling like he was being set up for something. Instinctively his defenses started to become alert, his "spidey senses" started tingling.

"I've kind of been hoping that you were, I don't know how to say this, the one....I guess."

Neko was caught completely off guard. He didn't know how to react. If this was a trick or a set up, he was clueless on how to respond. He had no idea what Chloe was doing, or why she was saying these things. She had never been so forward about her feelings like this. While Neko was flattered by everything Chloe was saying, he couldn't help but feel like she was stealing his thunder. He was the one that usually set the emotional tone. She was supposed to be reacting to him.

"When we were in the doctor's office today, I have to be honest with you; I was excited when he told me I was pregnant with your child. Now hold on, I'm not trying to trap you or anything. But after all that we've been through, everything that we've had to survive, I just feel like God is blessing us for the work we've put in by giving us something we can call ours. Something that we've made."

Chloe was starting to tear up.

Neko sat dumbfounded, mouth wide open. For some reason, Neko couldn't help but feel that Chloe's openness about her feelings was her breaking away from him. In the past when the two would have issues come up, be it an argument or just a decision that had to be made, Neko set the tone. He didn't care if she let him do it, which he sometimes felt, but after a certain point, it worked. It was like their survival formula to Neko, problems come up, he would tell Chloe how he thought things should go, and they would do it. This wasn't it. This wasn't how things were supposed to go. This wasn't how things usually worked. What was going on?

Chloe was speaking in calculated utterances. Speaking as if she knew exactly what point she wanted to get across, but was trying to find the words. Sentence by sentence, this terrified Neko. He felt as if he was standing before a judge as he/she was rendering a verdict. Powerless, his entire life in someone else's hands. Resentment was starting to form out of fear. He had no idea where Chloe was trying to take this conversation. But Neko was convincing himself minute by minute that he didn't like it.

"But I knew I couldn't get too excited alone. This type of news was made to be shared. I expected you to say something to me, anything. As we drove from the hospital, we sat in complete silence. The other times I've been scared Neko, but I told myself that next time God blessed us; we should take advantage of it. This baby is supposed to be born. But you said nothing. We drove home in silence, and then you passed out as soon as we got here, and you did it as if nothing had happened."

Neko started to speak, "Chloe I worked...."

"Wait Neko, I'm not finished," Chloe cut in with more than a hint of bass in her voice.

Oh no she didn't, Neko thought. He would be damned if she was going to shush him on a matter as serious as this one. He would not allow Chloe to dictate his life to him.
"I wanted to be mad at you Neko, I really did. I wanted to know how you could react so nonchalantly. I watched you sleep. You looked adorable. That's when I realized how much I loved you. I realized I can't carry anger towards you. Simply because you don't feel how I feel. Hell, I knew you would only tell me it was my decision anyway, right Neko?"

Chloe had a tear, a slow tear, moving at a turtles pace down the left side of her face.

Neko hated to see her cry. But for some reason he rejected every thought he produced to comfort Chloe. She was trying to trick him; she was trying to tie him down. She wanted him to cower to her "vagina monologue," he wasn't even sure if he was supposed to speak.

"I know you Neko, and by now you know me. I love you with all my heart Neko, and again, I know you love me as well. I know we usually follow your lead on things."

Neko took some solace in the fact Chloe was acknowledging how fucked up this conversation was. Watching Chloe cry though, Neko would consider it water under the bridge, and gladly accept Chloe's apology.

"But this is different Neko, this is our decision and honestly I'm sick of waiting on you to do the right thing. You're a good man Neko, I'm truly blessed. I would love to spend the rest of my life with you; I would be just fine with that. Better yet, I would feel lucky if that's exactly how things turned out. But I want more Neko. I don't want more in a man, just more from you. I want this baby Neko. And I'm not trying to tie you down."

Neko felt like he was on a reality show. She was reading his mind on every point he thought of. He felt small and insecure.

"I really want you to be with me on this, but I also understand that you may have different plans for your life. I don't want to argue, I actually want things as easy as possible for you. I want you to know I've decided to have this baby. I'm not changing my mind. From here, you have the option to stay, which is what I want, or go, which I don't."

Chloe paused, hoping to God she didn't word that wrong. The last thing she wanted to do was push Neko away. She understood he may not understand her actions at the moment, but she really hoped he would.

The two sat in silence for what seemed like eons, but only amounted to a few seconds. Then Neko looked her in the eye. Chloe melted with his gaze. She hoped he would understand how much stress she was under and just hold her. Neko opened his mouth, but no words came out. He finally gave her sound. She waited patiently. Chloe felt like her life was depending on what Neko said right now.

"You done?" Neko asked Chloe this, then got up and left the room.

CHLOE: in her own words...

I wish you would stop but I allow you to keep going
Secretly wondering how I've given you so much of my powers
How I've been fighting for what I want to be ours

I wish you would stop pretty sure my heart can't take much more
Pretty sure I want myself to be yours
Pretty sure I won't survive what I'm asking you for

I wish you would stop so hopefully I can move forward
Cuz everytime I try to leave I'm halted by your speech
As I've transformed your love from a want to a need

I wish you would stop let me go why don't you
Not trying to make you do things you don't want to
Cuz I would never want you going through what I'm going through

I wish you would stop and just be who you're supposed to be
The same as you were when you were approaching me
Say what you said when you first spoke to me

I wish you would stop let me stop kidding myself
I'd rather deal with pain of you
Than the love of somebody else....

CHLOE BRYANT

XII

Neko closed the door to the bathroom. Walked over to the mirror and stared at himself. He did not recognize the person he was looking at, he thought to himself that the Neko Rose that everybody knew would never have treated Chloe in such a way. He could hear Chloe sobbing in between his own thoughts but there was a lump in his throat and cement blocks around his ankles preventing him from coming to Chloe's aid. He felt like he had just delivered some tough love. He felt like he had to insure that Chloe understood he didn't respond well to ultimatums. Frustration began to settle in as he struggled to remember if Chloe had given him an ultimatum at all. But she had to have done it. Chloe had forced Neko's back against a wall. She had basically threatened him.

Right?

Hadn't she?

Neko started to feel a real uneasy feeling take over. He was starting to understand the gravity of this particular moment in time and what it may represent to the fabric of his life. He had just lashed out at Chloe, kind of. He was confused. She had tried to tell him how she felt and he took it and ran with it. She must be going through hell right now and he was punching the ticket.

"Neko Rose, you've really done it this time," he muttered to himself. His mind raced as he tried to figure out how to rectify this situation. What would he say? How could he possibly remove the foot from his mouth? This would prove to be more difficult than he thought because he still wasn't completely sure how he felt about the baby situation. He felt worse as he compared his confusion to what Chloe might be going through at the time. His soul mate was having her emotions rocked from side to side. He had to fix it, he just had to. He tried to gather himself. He ran to the faucet and tried to devise a game plan as the water warmed. He cupped a handful of lukewarm water and splashed it over his face. He looked into the mirror, but now with a sense of determination. He would fix this, he had to. He would, if nothing more, apologize for the callous way he had been towards Chloe.

As he turned the faucet off he heard a door slam. He opened the door to the bathroom and prepared to exit. Taking a deep breathe. He knew he would do a lot more listening. He would have to insure that he and Chloe were making the decision together. She did deserve more input than he was giving. He walked into the living room and began to speak before Chloe could even react to him entering.

"Baby, I'm sorry for what I...," he was halfway into his sentence when he noticed he had lost his audience. Chloe had left. She was gone.

XIII

Chloe sat behind the wheel of her car, sobbing. She couldn't believe what had just transpired. She had never been treated in such a way by Neko, and the two had had more than their fair share of heated exchanges. Lying, cheating, you name it, and regardless of the situation, they always maintained a sense of respect for one another.

Chloe was replaying the interaction in her head over and over again. Had she said something wrong? Could she have somehow provoked Neko? All she had wanted to do was convey to Neko how serious this situation was to her. She felt like her whole world was caving in, and shit was all good just a week ago. She felt weak, her eyes burned from the tears, not to mention she was pregnant. Now Neko was compounding this dreary situation with his careless attitude and blatant disregard for her feelings. Chloe wished she could make herself invisible.

When she was a child her grandfather used to always play a game with Chloe where he would take off his glasses and pretend not to see Chloe. They would scamper around as he would attempt to find her, with her uncontrollable laughter being a dead giveaway. But to her their game wasn't just a game. She reveled in the idea and the hypothetical power wrapped in the idea that she could make herself visible at her own discretion. She would run from one side of the room to the other and say, "Here I am grandpa," barely able to conceal her joy and enthusiasm.

Those days are gone now. These thoughts drift away as fast as they came. She was not a kid anymore, and her grandfather had long since passed away. Hell, she was on the brink of being a parent herself. She let her phone go to voicemail without even once glancing to see who it was. Even if it was Neko, she wouldn't be able to stand the sight or sound of him right now. No pep talk from Jazmine or Tanya would suffice right now. She couldn't even begin to start the car, she just sat.

Chloe and Neko had never left a conversation unfinished. It was something they had promised each other and they tried their best to practice this doctrine they had established. They loved each other, an idea that had never been questioned. They also knew the only thing capable of standing in their way was themselves, coupled with bad lines of communication. Each of them could probably spew off multiple times where they had conformed to the wishes of the other, all in all, sacrificing one's own belief for the pursuit of the perceived greater good. But what had gotten into Neko? Chloe was quite sure that Neko also was under a great deal of stress, but weren't they both? Her phone went off again. Now she was sure it was Neko. Somewhere inside, Chloe wanted to answer and talk her way back upstairs so the two could handle this situation the right way. In a matter of this magnitude, cooler heads needed to prevail. Chloe knew this but also knew it wasn't her that needed to take heed to this message. From her tears she recognized her own investment. Chloe wasn't easily rattled, although her demeanor sometimes didn't illustrate this fact. Chloe was about progress. She did what she had to do to get things done. And concerning her and Neko, sometimes this meant conceding to him. "When the grass is cut, the snakes will show," she remembered her grandfather always telling her. To Chloe this meant to keep things moving at all costs, and those that can't keep up will expose themselves. Trickles of anger creeped into her line of thought as her hands began to tingle. Her phone went off again. She was quite sure it was Neko at this point. But as of now she had no motivation to so much as hear what he had to say. She didn't want to argue or even hear a sorry attempt at an apology. It had finally dawned on Chloe that she had done nothing wrong, and she wasn't going to beat herself up or drag Neko along with this situation. She had spoken her piece and Neko had made it painstakingly clear there was nothing else to say at the moment. If Neko was going to act like an asshole, Chloe was quite sure she could do badly all by herself.

And with that thought, she started her car and began to drive away. She turned her phone off as it rang again. She was focused on getting anything to do with Neko off her brain. As she left his apartment, she turned around and caught an image of Neko's silhouette. She returned her head forward. Neko's the past, she thought. Chloe wanted to go forward, and she knew exactly where she was going.

XIV

"You've reached the Sprint PCS mailbox of….Chloe Bryant…," Neko pushed the end button on his cellphone. Chloe wasn't answering her phone. Neko was starting to get restless; it was driving him crazy that he couldn't talk to Chloe. The more he replayed the situation in his head, the more he wondered why this situation was being blown out of proportion like it was. He hadn't even been allowed to speak. The two words he was finally allowed to utter couldn't possibly have led to this. Neko was convinced all the two needed to do was talk this through. He tried her cell again…straight to voicemail. He pondered texting, and then decided against it. He needed to be able to look Chloe in the eye at this point. He paced around his apartment like he was looking for something he couldn't find. Although Neko wasn't exactly sure how this episode started, he knew how it ended. He wished he could just skip to the part where they were putting this episode behind them. Chloe probably wasn't going to let that happen, she had a way of milking situations for all that they were worth, and this would undoubtedly be no exception. Neko knew he would be the one to have to cater Chloe while she stomped around like a kid who had just had her bike stolen. Things never went this way when Chloe screwed up. She would say "I'm sorry" and then do that little thing that she always did. Actually, that worked for Neko the more he thought about it. His phone went off, and he answered without even looking at it, "where are you?"

"Right outside, you miss me?" But this wasn't Chloe. Neko wanted to hang up. He took a deep breath before he responded.

"What up?"

"Nothing, in the neighborhood, didn't see wifey's car. You still were going to the studio?"

"I'm not sure," Neko responded, "why, what up?"

"Nothing much, gotta fifth of Goose, wanna have a drink real quick?"

Neko knew this was code for 'do you wanna get fucked up tonight?

"Naw, I'm good," Neko said.

"What's the matter, you and wifey have a fight? I kind of figured as much, what with all the news today. Sure you don't need to relax, I can be very comforting."

Neko was not concerned with sounding enthused.

"How about a rain check, what are you doing tomorrow?"

"Look nigga, I'm downstairs! Get your panties out a bunch and come open the door. She must've of really fucked your head up."

"Alright, damn," Neko conceded.

He knew this was a bad idea, but what the hell. How much worse can it get? Chloe wasn't answering her phone. He might as well relax before he drove himself crazy. He decided to have a drink or two to take the edge off. Then he would give Chloe a call later after she had had a chance to cool off. Neko promised himself not to let his company deter his focus, and took another deep breathe before he opened the door. There was a knock, interrupting this thought process.

"Come on nigga, it ain't summer out here."

He chuckled from his side of the door. He opened the door to reveal Jazmine, his dip. She kissed him on the cheek, and then spun off him, letting herself in, making sure to let her perfectly round bottom rub against him. As she did this, Neko looked around as if anybody cared to be watching him. Then he closed the door. Neko knew this course of action would probably make matters worse, but like most men, decided that having his cake and eating it too wasn't the worst thing in the world, and proceeded anyway.

XV

Chloe had no idea what she expected of Garrett that night. Half of her wanted to give herself to him, not necessarily sexually, but more or less, see where his head was on the subject of him and her. Chloe had had it up to here with Neko and his immature antics. Chloe was in a lot of emotional pain and couldn't help but be drawn to someone familiar. Garrett wasn't the perfect man, wasn't even her man, but at least she knew what to expect.

It had been no problem arranging for the two to meet. As usual, it seemed like Garrett dropped everything he was doing when she told him she really needed someone to talk to that night. She wanted so very badly to let her guard down that night and although she knew she would never approach Garrett in that manner; she couldn't promise she would stop him if he tried. She was already picturing his soothing words and kind advice. Garrett had a way of telling her the brutal truth without being too demanding. He was always taking his time when he spoke to her. He would take long pauses after she spoke, letting Chloe know that he was listening and really thinking about what she had to say. His advice was always calculated and deliberate, not like her girls, who to their credit, always took her side. He told her what she needed to hear but was really, really smooth about it. Garrett was the only man Chloe knew that could get her wet with his words, without even mentioning sex or anything physical, yes, he was that good. "Dammit," she screamed aloud. She slowly reeled herself in from these thoughts. The stone cold reality was she was with Neko, pregnant with his baby, and she didn't get down like that. No matter how much she was pissed at Neko, she wasn't prepared to throw it away for the old 'grass is greener trick. Besides, she wasn't a home wrecker; Garrett was in a committed relationship, he was happy.

Chloe couldn't help but tease herself though on how grateful Garrett's wifey must feel with a man like him. She must really appreciate him, a man who knew what to do and didn't need training, 'praise Jesus. Chloe pulled up to the spot where they were meeting. It was an upscale lounge Garrett had shown her years ago. Garrett had a real sense of style, a modern renaissance man. She always felt like a scene from the movie Love Jones when she was with him. She parked her car and as she was walking up, she saw Garrett waiting for her. Chloe was twenty minutes early, Garrett must of flew over to the lounge.

Two cool points for Garrett.

They embraced. He was looking good, decked out in a black pea coat. Garrett was a red bone, with good hair. Must have Indians in his family Chloe always thought. He always kept himself neat and trim. He didn't wear baggy clothes. He actually dressed like he had some respect for himself. Tonight was no difference. He sported khaki's with a V-neck sweater and brown hiking boots. He looked good, although his ensemble looked like he wasn't even trying. Plus, you could smell cologne from only a few feet away. Chloe liked this; she hated guys who thought they should use half the bottle of cologne every time they put some on.

Two more cool points for Garrett.

He definitely knew how to get his grown man on.

"So what's the big emergency girl, you alright?"

Garrett asked this sympathetically. They strode into the lounge, proceeded over to a dimly lit corner and seated themselves. Garrett motioned over to the waitress, ordered a bottle of Moscatto, and instructed the waitress to make sure the glasses were chilled.

Two more cool points for Garrett.

The waitress left and the two got comfortable. 'My God, it's the little things, Chloe thought to herself. Chloe always noticed how when Garrett asked a question, he waited for her to answer. However long it took, however long she needed.

Two more cool points for Garrett.

"Same old, same old," Chloe started, "feeling like I'm alone in my relationship. I'm trying to take my time and be polite about the fact there are two people in a relationship. But this boy I got is trying my patience. Garrett, he really, really is."

Garrett's eyes never left hers. He listened to her like he had won a million dollars and she was giving instructions on how to claim his winnings. Garrett listened intently as she gave him the details on her and Neko's latest exchange. By her second glass of Moscato, he had begun to break it down to her. She was trying to make sense of what he was telling her.

"Oh, so you don't think I went too far, but I may have scared him a little bit huh?"

Chloe was trying to wrap her head around what a man might be thinking. He continued his analysis.

"Babe, men are thrown off when we feel we aren't given a choice, even though all you did was give him a choice."

The more Chloe thought about it, the more it made sense.

"Sorry to tell you this but we men suffer from a severe inferiority complex when it comes to women, and it never goes away. Hell if I'd known that then, maybe we'd still be together, sorry to admit that, but it's true, we men learn slowly."

Why did he have to say that, Chloe thought? She didn't know that Garrett even still thought about her in that way. She was blushing; she tried not to look so obvious, but couldn't control it. She was smiling, ear to ear, so much so that she had to excuse herself from the table.

She stepped into the ladies room and knew she had to get a grip. Her nipples were hard and she felt all warm inside. She started to remember what Garrett felt like, inside her. Chloe was contemplating if she could lose herself and blame it on the alcohol. She was telling herself that after her next glass she would leave, but all she was doing was proving to herself that even if she didn't do the right thing, she at least knew what it was. She started to playback the teary episode she had earlier. And it didn't take long before she concluded that "it" was Garrett's that one night, if he wanted it. She calmly checked herself out and left the ladies room. She focused on blocking Neko from her mind as she strode back to the table.

Garrett was on the phone, laughing as he spoke, he didn't notice Chloe. She was smitten with his smile. She swore he could be a Shemar Moore look-a-like. But as she got closer and began to be able to make out what he was saying, Chloe froze.

"Yeah, it's a wrap for tonight homeboy, its going down tonight. Hey, hey, what I tell you, if I hit once, I can hit again, just a matter of time. She in the bathroom now, had her open like a 7-11."

Chloe had to force her feeling of disgust for Garrett at that moment to take over if nothing more than as a mechanism to hold back the tears. Garrett had been playing her all along.

Minus two cool points.

All the while he was only plotting to have sex with her.

Minus two cool points.

Her emotions were nothing more than a game to him.

Minus two cool points.

Chloe fixed her face, walked up to the table and began to put her coat on. Garrett abruptly ended his phone call, startled by Chloe's imminent departure.

"Everything all right, you were in there for a minute."

"Everything's cool 'homeboy. I heard you and your ego on the phone, you fucking jerk!"

"Chloe wait!"

"Save it Garrett, be happy I'm not at your ass with this Moscato bottle right now. Toodles nigga."

Chloe stormed out of the lounge. Garrett didn't move a muscle. He actually just sat there, finishing his wine, eyeballing the waitress who had been serving him and Chloe all night. Chloe slammed her car door, burying her head into her steering wheel. She was tearing up. She was ashamed of herself and what she had been about to do.

"What a fucked up day," she thought to herself, "what else can possibly go wrong?"

XVI

"Ya'll can't see me on this spade shit. Rock up then!"

Neko professed confidently his acumen for the age-old card game. It was New Year's Day, two months previous, and Chloe was hosting a small get together for some of her and Neko's friends. A hearty party of eight or nine people, conversing and imbibing all while celebrating the New Year.

Neko and his tried and true partner on the spade table, Smoke, were handling Jazmine and Tanya pretty handily. Jazmine and Neko were well past full at this point and were throwing verbal jabs at each other left and right.

"See Jazmine, what you needs to understand is that these here spades are a man's game."

Neko speaks as he is dealing, staring directly at Jazmine, not once dropping his to watch the cards.

"But I understand if you wouldn't know nothing bout that, you know, a man, or having one, considering your track record. Maybe you should check the ingredients on your perfume, maybe it has dick repellent in it."

These are low blows, but for Neko and Jazmine, its par for the course. Jazmine, never shy about her ability to dish out as well as she receives retorts right on cue.

"You know Neko; you may be right, but uhh…What does that say about you? I mean if my perfume has dick repellent in it, we been sitting here for hours and you seem mighty comfortable, you and your, what do they call them, partner."

That one kind of stings Neko. But even Smoke can't help but chuckle a little bit, while Tanya is almost about to fall out of her chair laughing. Chloe, on cue and more than accustomed to her role as mediator, does her customary duty and sides with the underdog.

"Hey Jaz, my man is in fact all man, aint that right baby?"

"Don't worry baby, I don't acknowledge She-Devil over here. She has a voice that to a man sounds like a dog in heat and her breathe smells like boiled bologna. Why you think no man will come near her?"

Neko had killer instinct when it came to these types of moments, but Jazmine was no slouch.

"Chloe, stop taking up for your sorry excuse for a man. As for you Mr. Rose, don't front, we all know you was a virgin to skillful use of your tool before you met Chloe, and she was feeling sorry for you. She even told us how she had to teach you everything like a little puppy."

Jazmine adds in a little pantomime of a small puppy. Vulgar, but classic.

"Jazmine!"

Chloe screams, who at this point is doing a bad job of making it sound like she is actually taking up for her man, because she is laughing at the same time.

"True story?" Neko asks, staring down Jazmine.

"True story," she retorts.

The two are having one of those tense moments where no one in the room can tell if things are about to get ugly or not. Neko curls his upper lip, revealing a devilish smirk. He senses blood.

"Damn Jazmine, well if a grown man with no skills can find somebody, how that make you feel? Yeah, and Chloe told me how you had to have your cousin, Pierre, take you to your prom and all because the one dude that asked you decided to go with another dude. You must have really worked your magic on that one."

"Damn Neko, say it ain't so, that ain't happen, did it Jaz?" Smoke cosigns.

"Fuck you Smoke, and fuck you too Neko," Jazmine spews, "finish the damn game, what ya'll bidding?"

Neko refused to let the moment die.

"You mean this beat down Jaz, because this stopped being a game about two or three "yards" back."

This continued on and on like it usually does. Neko and Jazmine were stubborn which made for great comic relief at get-togethers. Around 11pm that night, the liquor was taking its toll; most of Neko and Chloe's guests had gone home. Only Smoke and Jazmine remained, Chloe had long since passed out, dead tired from a full day of playing hostess. Smoke had his eyes glued to the TV, watching a Boondocks marathon on Adult Swim, and did this without a care in the world. Neko was cleaning up while Jazmine was in the kitchen fixing her a plate to take home. Smoke, breaking from his trance only for commercials, approached Neko. Whenever he got drunk, he pestered Chloe and Neko about hooking him up with Jazmine. Contrary to Neko's analysis, Jazmine was a dime. The attitude only added to her mystique. She was one of the girls, as Smoke put, "who made you wanna grab they hair when you hit from the back." Smoke wasn't lying. Jazmine was a dark complexion, a pretty shade of chocolate. She was tall for a girl, about five foot and eight inches tall. She had long hair, and her body was, and always had been, a topic for discussion. People often wondered if it was "all her." Again quoting Smoke, "body was banging."

Jazmine didn't have trouble getting a man, but actually suffered from "which one." She wasn't shallow though, and had long since grown out of having to be the center of attention. But with this, also came pickiness. She didn't let just anybody spend time with her, and had absolutely no interest in Smoke.

"Neko, she been eye-balling me all night, I think she on it," Smoke whispered to Neko, "Put in the word, then bounce, you feel me?"

Smoke was talking in half speech, where half of his words were slurred. He was about to say something else, but lost his train of thought when Boondocks returned from commercial. Neko, not making sense of anything Smoke just said, continued cleaning up, working his way into the kitchen. He headed for the pantry to empty the trash and found Jazmine looking for aluminum foil to cover her plate.

"Stop trying to feed your cousins and shit with our food," Neko teased sarcastically. These two never stopped. Ever.

"Neko please, you should be happy somebody eating this nasty ass food you cooked. I bet roaches run away from this shit," Jazmine shot back.

"Whatever, here's a New Year's resolution, get a man. And if you having trouble, which it seems you always are, Smoke out there might, and I would have to check with him, might, settle for you."

"Negro please. I can have whoever I want," Jazmine responded as if directing this directly at Neko, indirectly. They both noticed noticed what was said, paused for a moment, and then attempted to squeeze past one another in the narrow pantry. Neko couldn't help but notice Jazmine slightly poke her ass out as he slid past. And he hoped she didn't notice that his dick was on hard. Jazmine tried to break the mood. But they both had noticed what had happened.

"Guess I can get a man. That's if you call your shadow, Smoke, a man."

Jazmine's attempt at humor went over dryly. Neko could only look down, because when he looked at Jazmine he noticed her nipples were hard in the shirt and bra she was wearing. He wasn't sure if he should try to squeeze back through. He was drunk, but not stupid. He knew that he and Jazmine were walking a tightrope right now and very close to falling off. He couldn't help but stare at this point, and Jazmine only noticed because she was staring back. Not wanting to be overt, she turned to allow his passage, but clearly made sure their bodies would touch when Neko exited the pantry. They were temporarily face to face as Neko did this. Neko paused directly in front of her asking, "Can I get by?" Jazmine's breasts were rubbing his chest. It was obvious they both were awaiting the others next move. "Go ahead," Jazmine replied. That was actually about the nicest exchange the two had ever had. Neko exited the closet. But Neko and Jazmine had officially entered each others primal thoughts and things would never be the same.

XVII

Chloe sat staring out her window pane, watching the rain drops scatter down her window. Dried up tears lined her face. She had long since lost the energy to even continue crying. She rhythmically jotted down poetry in her composition notebook. One of the reasons she was able to understand Neko's musical infatuation was her own with spoken word. It was therapeutic for her. Chloe had always been told she was mature beyond her years. She translated this to; she often exercised restraint and was not as quick to go off on somebody. Her notebook allowed her to cross that line. She never lacked confidence, but through her words she asserted herself. Today though she struggled. The pain she was feeling had induced writers block. This particular Saturday easily qualified as possibly one of the best and worst days of her life. She had found out that she was pregnant, again. Then after trying to have an adult conversation with Neko about it, she ended up catching the brunt of his, at times, stubborn attitude. She then found herself confiding in her ex-boyfriend, whom she considered a shoulder she could lean on, only to realize she was getting clowned because he was only trying to talk up on some ass.

Chloe was now trying to will the clock past twelve because she desperately wanted this day to end. She had considered calling Neko, but then decided against it after what had happened with Garrett. She felt guilty, but still didn't feel like confiding in Neko at the moment. Even though she had risked her fidelity that night, she was still pissed at Neko. The situation needed sometime to breathe, even if only until tomorrow. Maybe she would surprise him with breakfast, and then the two could start over with the conversation they had started earlier that day. She finally checked her phone. Neko had called her six times earlier. She wondered if he had wanted to apologize or still argue some more. You never could tell with him. She secretly feared Neko. She sometimes had no idea what to expect with him. She had never encountered a man who loved the way he did, but at the same time could bruise you with his words. His tongue was sharp. She had once seen Neko reduce a grown man to near tears with nothing more than an expletive laced tirade, stating nothing more than the facts. This was also the only man she knew of capable of bringing her to near orgasm with words. Oh yeah, Neko's tongue was definitely a weapon. She never understood how the two meshed. They could be complete opposites at times. Often you could find them on completely different ends of the spectrum. If one liked something, the other was indifferent. It was weird. Never so much as the two butting heads as much as if one liked something the other could care less about it. This allowed them to try new things. Chloe had turned Neko onto music even he hadn't heard of, and now had Neko reminding her of when the newest episode of The Kardashians was coming on. Neko in turn exposed her to movies she would never have considered and made her a true Chicago sports fan. Her affection for Derrick Rose was well documented, to the dismay of Neko. This was how they worked, however weird it was to everyone else and even them at times. They trudged along by their willingness to compromise and try new things with each other. But her happy thoughts were brief. She was pregnant now. And afraid she might possibly be on her won. What if her and Neko didn't work out? She was sure he would be a good father, but Chloe wanted a family. She wondered where Neko's head was on these subjects. She thought about Neko and what he was doing at that moment. She was calm, happy, upset, scared, sad, and confused all at the same time. She used her pain as her soundboard as she solemnly continued to stare out her window pane.

CHLOE: in her own words...

There's purple rain outside my window

Falling slow so I can see the color

A bueatiful dark twisted fantasy that I cant see from under my umbrella

Slipped and fell off

When I fell for your type

Wondering why it hurt so bad when it feels so right

The darkness makes it hard to see

The sex makes it hard to leave

But the fact that you could care less is what really makes it hard for me

Wake up and deal with the hearts hangover

Guess mines was built to be broken

My influence is influenced by the pain and cold shoulders

Hurry up and wait! They said

Where you going so fast?

Why your eyes so red? Maybe they just took a bath

Either deal or get dealt

Roll or rollover

If love is to walk on water then we rolled over the ocean

Not stealing thunder from the most high

Miracles are reserved

But in between our eyes I saw miracles observed

What I feel is beyond words

This is love but in reverse

Real as it gets this pain isn't rehearsed

Outsiders wanna check in

Offer condolences

Rather speak through a pen jump on some poet shit

Speak the real truth

So everybody know its me

This aint a love jones this is just my poetry

CHLOE BRYANT

XVIII

Somewhere across town, Neko sat and watched his girlfriend Chloe's best friend, Jazmine, sleep. He was trying to make sense of the mess he had created. He had been sleeping with Jazmine on and off for the past two months. After a chance encounter at a New Year's party, Neko had pursued her with little resistance from Jazmine. They both admitted they had no attachment to each other and was only in it for the thrill. The two would occasionally meet in discreet places, but lately Jazmine was making sure the two stayed in constant contact. A one-time thing was turning into Jazmine checking in with Neko every day. Tonight was how things usually worked. Jazmine had enticed Neko with a fifth of Grey Goose right after him and Chloe had had an argument. He secretly wondered if Jazmine had been aware of this. Either way, the more he was around Jazmine, he grew more and more curious as to why she didn't have a man, because truth was she really knew how to speak a man's language. She was submissive sexually, she allowed Neko complete control. She would keep things brief and to the point, and surrounded their encounters with "manly affairs." Namely, sports, alcohol, and sex. The more Neko thought about Jazmine, he sadly thought if confronted, his only reasoning could be she gave him what he didn't get at home. But Neko was starting to feel ashamed. He felt Jazmine was starting to get attached. The two had spoken that maintaining Chloe's confidence was the most important thing to them. They agreed that that things wouldn't get weird and their encounter was more explorative, kind of like a role play. Today was too much though, Neko hadn't touched Jazmine that night. This might have pissed her off or she was full before she got there. Either way she was slumped in the chair passed out. This left Neko sitting in his living room staring at his guilt with his mind racing on ways to patch things up with Chloe. But like most men, it never crossed his mind to tell Jazmine to leave, or how it might look if Chloe popped up. Like most men, given while in deep thought, he hadn't thought that far ahead.

He stared solemnly at Jazmine. She was pretty. Even prettier while sleeping. He knew Jazmine would jump in front of a moving train for Chloe. He would too. So what were they doing? Neko wasn't one to sugar coat; they were in essence having their cake and eating it too. He promised himself that he was cutting this thing with Jazmine, whatever it was, off. Fun was over, fantasy complete, back to reality. Things always got weird in situations like this, and right now was no exception. As soon as Jazmine woke up. He could explain it to her. The two agree that they had to focus on their love for Chloe and go their separate ways, hopefully no harm, no foul. He watched her sleeping and was pretty sure Jazmine would agree, underneath her nasty attitude she was pretty sensible. She must have been hearing his thoughts, because at that moment she smiled in her sleep as if to second his idea. She smirked and adjusted herself, knocking her purse over. Neko motioned to pick it up, knowing that Jazmine would have a fit if her designer Coach purse spent any time on the floor. Gathering the contents that had spilled onto the floor, Neko suddenly froze as if he had seen a ghost. Out of Jazmine's purse had fallen a pregnancy test. This was bad. Neko didn't immediately think the worst but he definitely was considering the implications. His stomach had dropped to his ankles. He knew he had gone "raw" once or twice with Jazmine. And even though he had pulled out, there was still a possibility....

He stopped himself there, afraid to continue entertaining the thought. This was bad, very bad.

XIX

Chloe awoke to the sun rising, still sitting next to the window overlooking the sky. She had slept peacefully and awoke with a renewed sense of purpose. She didn't necessarily feel like she had all the answers to her questions or problems, but she was re-energized with the strength to meet them head on. She glanced at her notebook to chronicle her thoughts from the night before. She did this often. To Chloe, written words or feelings were as good as photographs. They cemented moments in time. To her they were sometimes better than photos because of the details and descriptions involved. Her words left nothing to question, where as a photo caused you to guess what a person was thinking by their expressions. Chloe felt words got right to the point with no need for opinions or interpretations. Chloe secretly wished life could be this way. She wondered how much easier everything would be if life came with an instruction manual. It would definitely give her some insight on how to handle things with Neko. But being completely aware of these thoughts being nothing more than wishful thinking, she decided to go about things the good old fashioned way, hard work. With that in mind she set out to get ready for a day getting her life in order. Starting with Neko, she would tell him how much his opinion mattered and how much she thought it would help if they made this decision together. Most importantly, she would listen to Neko. Neko had hurt her in the past. She felt at times she had gotten too consumed with making sure he knew he was wrong and dragging him through mud when she had contributed to their problems. She wasn't conceding anything, but she was starting to figure out that spending so much time finding out who was wrong was counterproductive. At this point, who cared who was at fault for their problems, shouldn't her and Neko simply be concerned with getting to the bottom of them, more concerned with solutions? This was her new focus, meeting problems head on. Chloe took a very refreshing shower, felling re-invigorated and ready for action. She would surprise Neko and take him out to breakfast. She secretly hoped the public setting would go a long way in making sure her attempt didn't blow up in her face. She doubted if they would erupt into an argument at an IHOP. She dressed down and quickly, she was out of her apartment by 7:30 AM and on her way to her man.

She felt stability simply in the thought. A renewed sense of conviction. She was going to work for her man, and given the previous days revelations, her family. Wow, Chloe had never realized that right now, the seed inside her and Neko now constituted her immediate family. She couldn't let her mind wonder as she drove. There was traffic, and it was beautiful watching the sun take its place over the already breathe taking Chicago skyline. She daydreamed what life would be like. Chloe pictured their first Christmas, family vacations, birthdays, and soon had to reel herself in. she hadn't taken the time to notice how important family was to her until she felt it was being threatened as it was right now. As Chloe pulled into Neko's apartment complex, she had worked herself into a wonderful mood. She couldn't wait to see Neko, although she was prepared to deal with the flack she might catch for popping up so early. With Neko working nights at Power 92.3, anyone who knew him was fully aware that Neko wasn't a morning person. Never mind that, Chloe could currently think of quite a few ways to get Neko's attention no matter what time of day it was. God, she loved being a woman, she thought to herself. She actually wouldn't mind a little early morning wake up from her baby-daddy. She was smiling from ear to ear.

As she climbed the stairs up to Neko's apartment, she fumbled for her phone to call Neko to tell him to open the door. She stopped as she heard the chatter of a man and a woman, and thought to herself maybe she wasn't the only one up so early. As she approached she became more suspicious as she noticed the talking was coming from Neko's apartment. She focused on what she was hearing; trying to assure herself that it was indeed another woman's voice. As she listened intently she also noticed Trey Songz playing in the background softly. What was going on? She paused, noticing she had completely lost her breathe and she was feeling weak in the knees, but not in a good way. Her heart sunk. The morning of heartfelt ambition to preserve her relationship and future family was gone, suddenly replaced by a sense of shock with anger and frustration gradually coming up the rear.

Then the black woman in Chloe came out. She stormed to the door and gave it a good "police knock," one of those, "we know you in there" knocks.

"Open the fucking door Neko!"

All gracious formalities were gone. Chloe wanted to know what was going on, and she wanted to know now. She knocked again, while slowly mouthing a prayer for the home wrecker inside and what she was about to do to her. Neko wouldn't get off that easy, he was going to be tortured, literally. Chloe was livid.

"Open the fucking doors Neko, I already hear the bitch, I know she in there, might as well come clean," Chloe screamed.

She heard the locks being turned and she waited anxiously to see who Neko had risked their relationship for. The door opened. Standing there looking Chloe in the face was her best friend since she was a little girl, Jazmine.

Chloe couldn't breathe; the tears were coming fast and furious. She wanted to speak but the words just wouldn't come out, she just stood there shaking her head.

"You OK Chloe?"

Jazmine was speaking to her but all she saw was her mouth moving, she couldn't hear anything.

"You OK baby?"

Neko appeared at the door too.

"Baby?"

Why was he yelling Chloe thought? Chloe wanted to turn and leave but couldn't move. She tried to speak, but couldn't breathe. Then everything went black. Chloe fainted.

XX

Chloe came to in Neko's kitchen. It took her a few moments to get her bearings back. She was a little disoriented. Surrounding her was Neko, Jazmine, and Tanya, her other best friend. It was a pretty ironic situation. In that kitchen, at the moment, stood four people who had no idea what was going on and could do little for clarification. Neko, Jazmine, and Tanya wanted to know why Chloe had gotten so riled up and Chloe wanted to know why her best friends were at her man's house at 8 AM on a Sunday morning.

But first things first, everyone wanted to know if Chloe was OK. This overture to asses Chloe's health is what finally broke the inquisitive silence.

"Are you OK Chloe," Tanya asked, mirroring the sentiment of everyone in the room, including Chloe.

Chloe nodded, looking herself over as if doing her own mental evaluation in her head.

"I think so," she concluded.

But now that everyone was sure Chloe was OK physically, Tanya was the first to ask the other question everyone was thinking but not speaking about at the moment.

"Why were you at the door like a raving lunatic?"

Neko and Jazmine looked on intently; they had been giving each other weird eye contact that nobody noticed, as if they both had just had the same bad dream.

"I...." Chloe started, looking for the words.

"I don't know, I guess I got scared and angry when I came to the door and when I got to the door I heard female voices and the music playing."

"OK, that makes sense," Jazmine said, "but why did you go into shock when you saw me?"

Jazmine was tip-toeing a dangerous line. Neko instantly shot her a "what the fuck are you doing stare." Jazmine acknowledged him, non-verbally of course, and then returned her gaze to Chloe, awaiting an answer.

"I don't know," Chloe began, "I'm sorry Jaz. I honestly didn't flip because of you specifically; it was just the idea of another woman period."

Chloe was starting to get an idea of just how weird her episode came off to Neko and her friends. Neko, Jazmine, and Tanya all looked at each other. Then they all kind of nodded as if they got the same idea at the same time.

"Let me guess, you haven't checked your phone?" Neko asked this with a smirk emerging on his face.

Chloe let the question sink in, then gave a look of a kid asking an adult 'what do you mean Santa Claus isn't real. She reached for her phone, assured that she hadn't heard it go off, realized it was off, and turned it on. It sputtered as it vibrated wildly in her hand. She was flooded with alerts of text messages, calls, and voicemails, all from Neko, Jazmine, and Tanya. She took time to read one from Neko.

Really sorry about yesterday baby, me and your girls want to make breakfast for you, meet us at my place at 8, love you.

This text was followed by others searching for confirmation that Chloe had gotten the original text and wondering why she wasn't responding. Finally the last few were of concern.

U OK? We coming over.

The last one was from Tanya, five minutes before she had reached Neko's apartment. Chloe then finally noticed the aroma of the meal they had prepared for her. She also noticed that the kitchen table was covered with food wrapped up and that everyone had their coat on. She looked to Neko; her glance was one of a blind plea. She knew at this point he could be a little upset, and had every right to be, or he could understand. Chloe was hoping for the latter of the two. Neko sighed. He had one of those looks a parent makes when they know their child was wrong for something, but also knows that the child was only trying to help. It was a look of empathy. It was as if Neko was processing, wondering what he would do if he had been in the same situation. Would he have reacted any differently? He began to explain.

"Baby, I called you like 50 times last night. I'm sorry how I reacted. When I couldn't reach you, I hit Tanya and Jazmine to see if they knew what was up, I started to worry when neither of them had heard from you. I actually went by your house and saw you passed out in the window. That was when we all decided to get up early and make breakfast for you. But when you still didn't respond, that's when we decided to take the breakfast to you."

Chloe watched Neko's eyes confirm the validity of his story. This, coupled with the added reinforcement in the looks of Jazmine and Tanya, she suddenly started to cry again.

"I'm so sorry," she began, "I don't know what I was thinking. Oh my God, ya'll must really hate me right now, or think I'm a crazy bitch or both."

"I thought that anyway, that you were a crazy bitch," Tanya chimed in with a smile. Little did Tanya know that Chloe was speaking of this incident coupled with what had happened last night with Garrett.

Chloe felt horrible and truly blessed all at the same time. At that moment she felt she didn't deserve the people in her life, this sincere and loving group that she had. Chloe reached for Neko, hugging him.

"I'm so sorry baby."

She was still teared up. Neko's arms and body consumed her, as she hid her head in the crevice where his chest was separated from his arms. Tanya continued with attempts to lighten the mood.

"Neko alright," Tanya said sarcastically, "but never worth what me and my girls got."

Chloe laughed, while Neko and Jazmine shot each other quick glances. Things were officially starting to get weird.

XXI

"I can't believe I thought you had another woman in here, let alone Jazmine," Chloe mused.

Tanya and Jazmine had left Chloe and Neko alone to discuss their issues.

"I know right. You gotta give me more credit than that. Jazmine of all people?"

Neko fired back quickly, although his stomach was in knots. Chloe and Neko were miring themselves in a superficial mess. They both were secretly breathing sighs of relief that their infidelities hadn't caught up with them, and were thankful that they would have a chance to make things right with one another, because they truly did love each other. But they had yet to dig into the heart of the matters they faced, Chloe was pregnant and they had no idea what they were going to do. It seemed as if right now they were being polite. The "I love you baby" exchanges were free flowing. This was a far cry from just 24 hours ago. Finally Neko decided to speak from his heart.

"Baby, I watched you sleep last night. In your window. You were so peaceful. That's when it dawned on me that I was afraid. I'm afraid I won't be able to provide that peace. That fear is what causes me to keep you at a distance. I figured with more time I could make a way for me to provide that peace I want for you. And all this is before we even think baby. I'm terrified to see if I can provide peace to a baby. I'm ashamed though at how I've went about things, how I've spoken to you. I turned my fear into resentment towards you because I know it's something you've wanted all along; you know the baby and all. And you just always seem so sure about everything. And that feeling hurts two ways because for one I feel like a jerk because I don't have a clue and two, you'll expose me and realize you don't need me anyway. And I just don't know if I can handle that so...."

Neko was starting to break down. Chloe saw this and rushed over to console him. She hand never seen him be so open about his feelings. She had also never felt more in love with this man as she felt at that moment.

"I want this baby, and I want it with you, and I want you, and I want it to be an us."

With these words from Neko, Chloe began to cry. But she also was overwhelmed. She felt so guilty about her previous evening with Garrett. She knew how close she had come to saying the hell with Neko. She knew she had been Garrett's for the taking. But now she sat in the arms of a man she felt truly loved her to her core and she had almost thrown it away. And she felt pained by this emotional overload. She couldn't share with anyone. It was tugging at her soul and ripping her apart at her very core. She had been on Neko to be more of an ideal she had created, not noticing that he was more. She noticed she had been comparing him and what she thought she wanted to a man that didn't exist. His admission was that of a man at the end of his rope, exhausted from her little games, sounding as if he didn't even know who he was anymore. All this and she had been on the verge of confiding, both physically and mentally, in another man. Chloe was devastated, and could no longer carry this weight she abruptly got up and ran to the bathroom, turned, locked the door, and immediately fell to the floor in tears. She had reached her wits end. Neko was powerless.

This is what he had been referring to. He didn't know how to fix these types of problems. He couldn't help Chloe right now. He didn't even know what was wrong. He was frozen. Him and Chloe were in a lot of pain but were on opposite sides of the door, both physically and mentally. But what was that noise. Was it in Neko's head? There was a vibration he couldn't escape. He wondered if it was his head about to explode. Finally, he realized it was Chloe's phone. He picked it up to silence it but couldn't help but notice the text. It was from Chloe's ex-boyfriend Garrett. He wanted to apologize for last night. He hadn't meant any disrespect. He wanted her to know he loved her, and it was just fine that things didn't get physical. What was going on?

Neko didn't have the strength. He let the phone drop to the floor. Never even bothering to silence it and he just sat there. Eyes glazed, completely inept, and on account of Chloe's phone, left with the ground shaking.

XXII

"How are we ever going to know if we can fly if we don't jump out of the plane?"

Neko propositioned Chloe. At the moment the two took flight. Neko and Chloe had only been dating, at the time, for a couple of weeks. Its Labor Day weekend, Neko has some free passes to Six Flags Great America. Neko has been on a day long quest to to get Chloe to take some chances on various roller coasters. He'd been fairly successful up to this point, but the bungee jump attraction he'd talked her into has to stand as his crowning achievement for the day. Chloe isn't terrified of heights but she is partial to keeping two feet on the ground and is nowhere near as geeked up about things as Neko is. She also understands how Neko is using her unwillingness to go on rides as a metaphor for her reluctance to let herself go with Neko emotionally.

At this point they had shared themselves with each other and there definitely was something there. They both couldn't argue they had "grown sweet" on each other quickly and were catching heat from their closest of confidants about going too far too fast. Neko, a self-described risk taker didn't seem to mind. He figured if the two were on the same page, there was no harm in embracing their feelings. For the life of him he couldn't figure why anyone would decide to spend less time with someone they really liked, simply on the idea of maintaining the status quo, or not wanting to put yourself out there. He likened it to going to a buffet to pick at the food on your plate. Neko had christened this idea on his and Chloe's first date. He joked with her at the restaurant they went to that he wasn't into girls who didn't eat.

"Don't complain about a brother never taking y'all nowhere nice if y'all just gone pick at your food."

Chloe could only smile as she nibbled at her chicken tenders. Neko had a way about him where he could rub you the wrong way, he was set in his ways and to some this could be construed as stubborn or confrontational. Chloe recognized this about him immediately, and while she didn't find it sexy, per say, it made her laugh. In fact the reason Neko and Chloe enjoyed each other so much is mostly due to their differing opinions and ways of doing things on just about everything. They would talk for hours on in about the most mundane things, amazing themselves at how the other drew their conclusions. For example, Neko didn't understand why Chloe was so apprehensive about the status of their relationship. Key word for Neko being "status." Chloe and Neko were quite clear on the "nature" of the relationship, meaning they knew it was something special and serious, which Neko called "the three S's." But the two would playfully banter about the status. Chloe felt if they were on the same page, why rush to define everything and add titles. This segued into her past. Her last relationship had taught Chloe not to jump head first with her emotions. Her last relationship, between her and a guy named Garrett had left scars that Chloe was still recovering from. Chloe had invested her all, and was actually shocked she was able to carry on with Neko the way she did. The fact that she was cautiously proceeding was a testament to the "nature" of the relationship her and Neko were developing. They never set out to suffocate each other, but time just seemed to fly when they were with each other, and they genuinely enjoyed spending time together. This left them in a place, again, which exemplified the dynamics of what they had. Even their disagreements ended casually with the only stalemates being chalked up to bad lines of communication. But 99.9% of the time, they were left with the fact-this subject also being the case-that they were both right. Neko understood that Chloe was tentative about their relationship because of Garrett, while Chloe could see that they were in a relationship, if not in title then definitely in nature. So as Chloe sat strapped to Neko, still wondering how she allowed herself to get talked into this one. She felt her nervousness subdued as Neko whispered to her, "no matter what, I got you."

XXIII

Neko knocked on the bathroom door. Chloe responded, "I'm sorry baby, I just needed to wipe my face." Neko knocked again. "Baby, I'm OK, really, I'll be out in a second." Neko knocked a third time. This time Chloe opened the door, "what's wrong, do you have to use the bathroom?" But immediately Chloe noticed the look on Neko's face wasn't one of having to use the bathroom. It was actually a look of bewilderment. A look of not understanding, coupled with not wanting to understand if he did understand.

"Neko's what's wrong, are you OK?"

Chloe looked concerned. But as Neko looked at Chloe he was beginning to not recognize her. Neko knew every curve of Chloe's face. But by the second her face was becoming unfamiliar to him. Biblically, Chloe had just eaten the apple in Neko's eyes. Neko and Chloe had always been jealous about one another but never seriously considered the other was stepping out. Usually they argued about what one of them thought the other "might" do. There had never been clear cut evidence that either one of them had cheated. Neko though, over their relationship had placed symbolic ownership of Chloe. More in an "I'm proud of the woman I have" kind of way, as opposed to a domineering kind of way. Now he boiled with the thought that Chloe could have been "sharing." As all these thoughts rushed through his head, he sat there as Chloe continued to ask what was wrong, finally he spoke.

"Garrett says sorry about last night, that he loves you, and that he's OK if things didn't get physical."

Garrett, in just a matter of hours, had turned himself into someone Chloe really was wondering if she cared to ever see again. Chloe wore this thought on her face. Neko took this look as Chloe being disgusted with Neko going through her phone. Neko was holding her phone up so she could read it. Chloe cringed and Neko's expression was one of a wounded puppy.

"OK," Chloe thought, wanting to choose her words very carefully at this point.

"Neko, let me explain," is what she came up with.

A look of disgust shot upon Neko's face. Wrong answer. She might as well have said "what had happened was." Neko was a bullshitter, true story, but he didn't like to be bullshitted. Neko reasoned that if someone was telling the truth it didn't go that way. To Neko this was the course of action you got from someone who was making a story as they went along. Honestly, Chloe was debating what and how much to tell Neko. She had been out with Garrett, and she was happier than anyone that nothing had actually happened. There was really nothing to tell but she knew that wouldn't work for Neko. He was trying to be patient. His patience was wearing thin though. He finally asked the question that was burning within him.

"You fucking him?"

These words cut into Chloe like a knife.

"No, Neko. I haven't fucked anybody but you," Chloe shot back.

But that question had been a lose-lose situation and Chloe knew it. If she had said yes she was doomed and it was apparent that Neko wasn't satisfied with the true answer she had just given. Chloe, between the chaos, was amazed at how fast the tables could turn. Just hours ago, Neko was groveling at her feet to regain favor with her. Although she wasn't trying to dodge the issue, Chloe did wonder what the day would have been like had she simply slept in. she wasn't trying to downplay the issue but she didn't know exactly how to explain to Neko there was nothing to Garrett's text. Neko's tone was rising gradually but still at this point, somewhat subdued.

"Why is Garrett, your ex-boyfriend if I remember correctly , apologizing for last night, and saying you two are OK even though you didn't get physical last night?"

"Neko that's not what it sounds like," Chloe said matter-of-factly.

"Then by all means, explain it to me Chloe. I'm listening."

Before Chloe could even respond, Neko continued.

"If I'm not crazy, this lets me know you and him were together last night, that there is still something going on because he's "cool" if things didn't get physical last night. What about other nights Chloe?"

"I'm not fucking him Neko. I have no plans to fuck him," Chloe was getting heated. It was obvious by the inflection in her voice. "Me and Garrett had a drink and I went home, alone. I went to sleep right where you say you saw me passed out in my window."

Neko jumped right on the statement like the two were arguing in court. "Let me get this straight, the day we find out your pregnant, of all the people you can talk to, you talk to your ex? Ignoring my calls in the process. Not to mention, you were drinking alcohol."

However harmless the evening had been with Garrett, Chloe knew Neko was right. She wasn't trying to argue, she would much rather say she's sorry after explaining everything, or almost everything. That might not be possible right now, Neko was pissed. Chloe would consider it a victory if her and him could make it through this conversation without saying something hurtful but this would be tough, but now Chloe's blood pressure was slowly building as she was being drilled and answering questions that assumed guilt. Not to mention if Neko hadn't been such a jerk about everything yesterday, then her and Neko would have spent the evening discussing their issues. This was turning into an episode of "When keeping it real goes wrong."

Neko felt Chloe was doing a whole lot of tap dancing without saying what was going on. This to him was a clear indicator of the fact that something was going on. All he could picture was another man inside Chloe. Neko was in a lot of pain. All he could think at this point was to make sure Chloe could feel exactly what he was feeling. He pulled out his phone and started texting.

"Neko?" Chloe wondered what he was doing.

He ignored her, continuing to text. He stopped, tossed Chloe her phone, and said, "Now you'll know how it feels." Then he walked away.

"Neko?" Chloe followed him into the living room. Neko plopped onto the couch and turned the TV on as if the last ten minutes with Chloe had not just happened. Chloe's phone went off. She checked it, still unsure what was going on. It was a text from Neko. As she read it, her face turned red. She finished reading, and then took a second to take it all in. then as if a light switch was turned on, Chloe Bryant went nuts. She attacked Neko, hitting him as many times as she could. Neko restrained her, careful not to retaliate. Chloe growled, yes growled. Neko held her, and she resisted furiously. Finally, Neko said, "you cool?"

She had calmed down or either was getting ready to go again. Chloe was crying now. He let her go and she did walk away, picked up her phone and walked into the kitchen. She read the text again, and continued sobbing.

I hope this is really my baby. Guess we'll have to see. Oh, and by the way, I am fucking Jazmine....but I can explain.

XXIV

"Is it true Neko?"

Chloe emerged from the kitchen an hour later. Dried tears lined her face.

"Is it true Chloe?"

Neko responded with extreme hints of sarcasm.

"Why are you acting like this Neko?"

Chloe was basically pleading with Neko. But she could not overcome his wall of pride. Chloe crumbled where she stood. To her knowledge, she had never felt pain like this. In just over twenty-four hours her life had been turned upside down. She still proceeded with the little strength she had left to communicate with Neko.

"Can we talk this out Neko, or are you not speaking to me?"

"Alright Chloe, what do you have to say?"

Neko responded again heavy on the sarcasm. Chloe was approaching her wits end, "do you just want me to leave?"

"What for Chloe, I thought we were talking?"

Neko continued to respond dryly. Chloe didn't have a clue and Neko was being an asshole. Chloe turned to leave; Neko was watching her, as if to see how far he had pushed her, how far would she go, and if she would ever come back. These two young lovers, after the time spent and the countless hours talking, still didn't understand each other's pain. They were falling prey to the superficial communication that most young couples suffer through. La La Land seemed very far away. Chloe was calculating in her head if she should stay or go. She took herself back to the morning and the vigor she felt to fight for her family at this point, pain now almost unbearable, she was intent on accepting the fact that she couldn't understand Neko's pain. But she also wanted to make clear that the strength between the two was misunderstood as well.

"OK Neko, you want the truth? I understand I may have hurt you and pushed you into a corner yesterday. I may have been wrong for how I presented my ideas to you. But I didn't know what else to do. I may not be able to take another abortion physically. I couldn't bear the idea of sharing this decision with you and all you being able to come up with is that you'll support me whatever I decide. That's not enough Neko. So I tried something else. After watching you ignore me on the day we get this info, sleeping all day, then watching a basketball game, I figured I would make it easy for you, or so I thought. This seemed to piss you off even more."

Neko was listening, actually ready to cut Chloe off, but as she continued to speak her decibels also rose. Even with things fractured the way they were, Neko knew to keep quiet. Also Neko had not been a complete jerk. He really did want to hear what Chloe had to say.

"Sometimes when I'm with you Neko, when it comes to put up or shut up time, I feel like I'm on my own. You hide behind this wall of if things aren't going Neko's way, then fuck it. That again is not how things work. I left here frustrated and yes I met Garrett for a drink. We had never met for a drink before this. Because me and you had never got to point like this. While there with him, I figured out he was on bullshit, so I left. True story. He must've texted me to apologize because I did tell him about his self. I have no inkling to make this more of a fucked up situation than it already is. Which is more than I can say for you."

Chloe's voice was raised at this point. As she explained things to Neko, she was also explaining things to herself. As the words rolled off her tongue, it made her angrier that she was explaining this to the boy. This spoiled brat, that she had done nothing wrong.

"I'm sorry for how I handled things. I have been, and had hoped we would figure this out, together. I'm sure I could have done some things differently, but I've never not wanted us to work. I've never not wanted your child. I don't know how hurt you are or the extent of what you are going through, but I've done nothing to add to it. I also don't know what's up with you and Jazmine. Honestly at this point, I don't even care. I only care about this baby, and for all I care, you and Jazmine can fuck each other's brains out."

With that said, Chloe left. Neko didn't move, as if he were getting her monologue on tape delay and was still listening. He didn't know what to make of it, and like most men, he just sat, waiting for something to happen, unaware that it just did.

XXV

Chloe got in her car and wondered where she was going. She had no idea who she could talk to, or who she could trust. Neko had just broken her. She was kidding herself if she thought the emotional haymakers he had just dropped could be chopped up to dirt on her shoulder that she could just wipe off. Garrett, her ex, and someone else that she confided in had revealed himself to be all fake, just another "nigga" trying to talk up on some ass. He had really tricked Chloe; she had actually thought the two were true friends. And then there was the ultimate deception. Her best friend Jazmine had been with Neko. Chloe hadn't had a chance to speak with Jazmine on this, and was wondering if she even wanted to. Furthermore, she wondered if Tanya, her other best friend knew anything about it. She was pondering if there was anybody that she could trust or was she just an inside joke to everyone she thought cared about her.

Chloe had never felt so alone in her life. She rubbed her stomach, and grew weary even trying to think how she might get through this. She knew she had to; she would have to be strong for the child. Chloe was well aware that what didn't kill her made her stronger, and like people usually say, "one day you'll look back and you'll laugh about this." It sure didn't feel that way. The foundations for her life, going back to childhood had eroded. She questioned what was sacred since obviously friendship, love, and loyalty were looking like nothing more than punch lines at the moment. How long had Garrett been plotting, how long had Jazmine and Neko been sleeping around? These people she trusted, that she spoke with almost daily, the whole time had been looking her in the face and basically lying to her. They spoke of love, and having her back, and always being there. But at this tough time, probably the most stressful time in Chloe's life, they had all been exposed as phonies. Where was the love? The more Chloe thought about it, the more numb she became to the idea. She had the symptoms of being in a state of shock. She was checking out, turning herself on auto-pilot. Maybe that way she wouldn't have to deal with the pain. But what about the baby? Snap back to reality to Chloe. Everything in her wanted to give up. She had chosen her friends and lover unwisely. Now she was suffering for it. There was no time for Chloe. They hadn't had time for Chloe. Now even Chloe didn't have time for Chloe. She had to put her feelings to the side and begin to come to grips with the fact she was pregnant. Life was going on whether she wanted it to or not. She had to be strong for her child. She was afraid, picturing herself on a milk carton, missing. Visualizing young people her own age, laughing to themselves asking, "whatever happened to Chloe?" she was riddled with self-doubt, wondering how she would pull through this. She suffered from the idea of being too weak. She hadn't been beaten, abused, and was in pretty good health. Other women were going through much worse. She was sure. So why couldn't she deal? She was a young woman with nowhere to be and nowhere to go, expecting a child, and that child would no doubt be expecting a mother that knew where to go and where to be. How could she kid herself into thinking that she was ready for all this? If her closest friends hadn't lowered her spirits to the depths of depression, Chloe Bryant was now doing it to herself. She sat there with all these thoughts racing through her head, starry eyed, but in reality she was going nowhere fast.

XXVI

Jazmine sat watching Chloe, her best friend from her car. The two had been best friends since they were kids. The two didn't necessarily share the same ideals, but for over twenty years of friendship they had never had a serious falling out. The two shared a mutual respect. Confident individually in themselves, they respected each other and stayed in their own respective lanes. And the usual lightning rods for young, attractive women, men and attention, had never been an issue. The two had helped each get and forget potential love interests, and was always at one another's side. They sacrificed for each other, understanding how important true friends were. If Jazmine wanted someone or something and Chloe had it, in terms of men, and wasn't that serious about him, she would concede to Jazmine. Vice versa, reciprocally. The two had their own ways about getting things done but glowed about the others ability to actually get things done. One's flaw was the others strength. If Chloe was being too sensitive, Jazmine would emerge as the aggressor. If Jazmine was being too ghetto, Chloe would add a more articulated insight to a situation. After both had been witness to young, beautiful women constantly cat fighting and pulling each other down, the depth of the girls' relationship was actually something to marvel at. But anyone who knew the girls, namely Tanya, would wince at what she was watching right now.

Jazmine watched Chloe, in clear discomfort, from the parking lot of Chloe's boyfriend Neko's apartment. Jazmine and Neko had embarked on an all too brief, for Jazmine, affair. It had only taken one time with Neko for Jazmine to figure she wanted more. While Neko previously threw jabs at Jazmine about her inability to find a man, she unfortunately had set her sights on Neko. Jazmine and Neko had tested the waters after sparks flew secretly at a New Year's get together. Although both acknowledged there was mutual attraction, their love for Chloe ruled out any ideas of infidelity initially. While she was supposed to be ignoring these feelings, Jazmine quietly allowed them to fester. Soon she had convinced herself that the only way to get these thoughts out of her head was to actually act on them. She figured by getting the act-that she knew was on the tip of her and Neko's tongue-out of the way, the two could move on, no harm and no foul.

She devised an elaborate plan of seduction centered on her catching Neko at the studio with someone to buy a beat from him. She enlisted one of the endless numbers of young, aspiring rappers out there, and duped them into meeting with Neko. The plan was actually quite effective. Neko, inebriated as usual at the studio, was no match for Jazmine's subtle but not too forward advances, as well as the heightened sense of testosterone Neko felt about selling one of his beats. Neko felt like the man at the moment, and all Jazmine had had to do was stroke his ego, among other things. Besides Neko was no match for Jazmine in a pair of low rise jeans and a fitted sweater. At that time, Neko's flesh was weak, and all Jazmine had had to do was casually brush against him. Soon, she felt his member, after manufacturing this moment, in the engineers sound booth. Although Neko invested no emotion in the act, the disconnect allowed for an almost animal like experience that Jazmine happily remembered and Neko quickly forgot. Upon climax, the two agreed that what they had done had to be a one-time thing, which turned Jazmine on even more.

She grew intent on causing Neko to go back on his idea. She would call and text. She would send pictures of herself in compromising positions. She was never pushy or stalker-like, but she made it quite clear to Neko that she was open to round two. Neko, was riddled with guilt, actually looked at the event as an opportunity to draw him and Chloe closer together. He began to appreciate what he had. But being completely aware of the problems a woman's scorn could create, he always kindly rejected Jazmine's overtures. Polite enough that she had yet to get he wasn't interested. Polite enough that she was growing more and more bold in her pursuit of Neko. Polite enough that she might be pregnant, and actually thought that Neko would leave Chloe for her.

She had tried to bring it up the night before when she had popped up at Neko's house, but Neko could do nothing but talk about Chloe. Jazmine eventually passed out in his living room, unbeknownst to her that Neko had found her positive home pregnancy test. She was growing obsessive in her attempts to get Neko alone, and this found herself posted up outside Neko's apartment waiting for his girlfriend, her best friend Chloe, to leave. She had come to a point where she knew what she was doing was wrong, but was making it make sense to herself. She rationalized, if Chloe didn't know how to recognize what she had and treat it properly, she would. Her phone vibrated, it was a text from Neko. Jazmine grinned, a devilish sort of grin, as she read...*she knows*.

In her eyes, now it was every woman for themselves at this point.

XXVII

Neko watched Chloe from the window of his apartment. He was still a bit disoriented from their last encounter. He had admitted to Chloe that he had been intimate with her best friend Jazmine, and upon hearing that she secretly rendezvoused with her ex-boyfriend Garrett, questioned if the baby she was pregnant with was actually his. Although he knew it was baby, he couldn't stop the rage he felt when the thought of Chloe being with somebody else might be reality. Regardless, of all the wrong he had done to her in the past. He wasn't sure if he would ever be able to forgive Chloe. Chloe had admitted the details of her encounter. Neko felt she was telling him what he wanted to hear, that she hadn't done anything wrong with Garrett. It bothered Neko just as much if she had done anything with the guy as it did that she had put herself in the predicament for something to happen. The fact that she met the guy in secret after ignoring Neko's calls was infuriating. If she had done this behind his back, what else had she done?

This bothered Neko more than anything else, not so much the physical deception as the mental. For Chloe to be Neko's woman, he had built her up in his head. She had become more than other women, physically, mentally, and morally. While daily he watched firsthand the evil that men do to the women who let them, he assigned an invisible force field around Chloe. She was immune to the shallow advances of all the thirsty brothers out there. She had the where with all to know that guys were only up to one thing, the goodies. Not only did she know this, but she also had Neko to protect her in assigning Chloe this knowledge, Neko himself had taken responsibility for her. Chloe's frequent submissive behavior to Neko had fed his ego. He had decided Chloe needed him. After this revelation with her ex-boyfriend, Neko felt small, like a pawn. This was her ex for God sakes. It could have been anybody but him in Neko's eyes. He had already experienced Chloe. He had been her first. In Neko's experience, women receive men when it comes to sex. Men leave their mark. If men do it well enough, they can always come back to that woman, off the strength of her own memories. Neko deduced if anybody had a chance to break Chloe down, it would be her ex. His ego told him he had prepared her, but he had failed. What he thought was his, wasn't. He was just another guy. Chloe had not understood when Neko had tried to explain all this to her. She had not been able to wrap her head around the idea of how territorial guys are. It amazed her how men could "stick their dicks in anything," as she put it, and then still have the nerve to catch feelings if a woman did the same. All Chloe could see was a double standard.

All these thoughts coursed through Neko's brain at the moment. His memories were working against him. His memories were telling him, that Chloe argued it was a double standard because she was guilty. The more Neko allowed the thoughts, the more he convinced himself that, however sorry he was for what he had done, Chloe had got nothing more than a dose of the same pain she was dishing out. Neko felt if ever there was a double standard, it was women when they assumed because we liked sports and video games, that men didn't feel pain. Just because a man doesn't carry on gossiping about relationships twenty four hours a day, does that say they don't care? Was Neko supposed to simply look past the fact that his girl had stepped out on him simply because afterwards she was deciding to tell the truth? Women would drag men through the mud, with long memories, never allowing men to live down their past transgressions, while women felt all they had to was give up an "I'm sorry" and maybe some head. Neko resented the fact that Chloe thought, college education and all, that all he thought with was his "little head." Neko purposely wanted Chloe to feel what he felt, every bit of pain of knowing what was thought to be yours was actually someone else's. He wanted her to hurt. He wanted her to have to deal with picturing him with someone else to see just how bad it felt.

Neko's rollercoaster thoughts were interrupted by his phone going off. He secretly hoped it was Chloe. He actually wanted to continue the conversation so he could drive home his points even further. He walked away to grab the phone. It was only Jazmine returning his text. Neko was underwhelmed. He had almost forgotten about her. Poor Jazmine, he thought, little did she know she was nothing more than a pawn for his attempt to get back at Chloe. Neko was curious and wanted to question her about the pregnancy test he had found. He was quite sure he had been careful. There was no way Jazmine was pregnant, let alone by him. Neko had to chuckle to himself as he thought how much worse this situation would be if Jazmine was pregnant. He read her text. She wanted to know Chloe's reaction to finding out about him and her. Neko didn't have time for this at the moment. His issues with Chloe took precedent. At that moment he heard a knock. He sighed as he felt his misguided attempt for attention had worked. Chloe was at his door he thought. She was ready to pardon him on whatever he had done because two negatives equal a positive. She would understand through her own actions that what he had done, while not ok, was a reaction, not an action. Neko, taking a bit of pride in the fact his plan had worked so smoothly, would have loved to pat himself on the back. As he strolled past the window on his way to open the door, he noticed Chloe's car was gone. Had Chloe left? He suddenly felt deflated. If Chloe wasn't at the door then who was it? Just then his phone rang, was it Chloe?

XXVIII

Tanya was sitting on Facebook in her room across town. She still lived with her mother, but not because she didn't have her stuff together. Tanya probably was the most well off of the three girls. She had decided to stay at home to help her mother with her younger brother and other issues that arose in her close knit family. Tanya was the glue that held most social circles she participated in together. She was as good for good advice as she was for help on bail money. She could quote scripture or put in on a fifth. She could easily be the life of the party, or babysit your kids if you wanted to go to one. Although Jazmine and Chloe had known each other for few years before Tanya came around, Tanya had carved her own niche within the group. Subconsciously, Jazmine and Chloe felt no threat from Tanya in regards to the issues most young women squabbled about, men.

Tanya wasn't a hobbit, but she couldn't quite command the attention that Chloe and Jazmine could. She was about five foot, eight inches tall, which was a bit tall for a woman. She was not as well-proportioned as the other girls. Quite frankly, she was skinny. Hadn't quite filled out, and her face was plain. She was normal. She was never the worst looking woman in the room, but she didn't naturally stand out either.

The beauty of Tanya lay in her ability to quickly and fairly access situations and her ability to listen. She always gave you her undivided attention when you dealt with her. She would make you feel as if your issues were more important than her own, sincerely. So while most young women focused on getting their hair done and how their butt looked in a particular pair of jeans, Tanya was too concerned with handling her business or helping you handle yours. When Chloe and Jazmine encountered Tanya, way back in the sixth grade, this was apparent then, and the three clicked immediately. They balanced each other out. Like branches of government, one watching the other, but three separate entities, all too busy in their own respective lanes to step into one of the others.

Tanya was proud of the bound the girls shared. She was proud of how the women continuously survived while most cliques's destroyed themselves from within. Her friends handled business; think Waiting to Exhale circa present day. Little did she know the very existence of the women as a group was about to be thoroughly tested. As Tanya scrolled through miscellaneous Facebook profiles, she immediately was stopped in her tracks by a photo that she knew would throw everyone the women knew up in arms. Without hesitation, she picked up the phone and called Chloe. No answer. Which kind of made sense after all her and Neko were going thru, she was sure they were tied up with each other. She then tried Jazmine, no answer. Knowing Jazmine, she was probably sleep. Although she would never admit it, Jazmine was obviously the one in the group who made beauty sleep essential. Tanya was beginning to get a bit worried though. From what she was looking at, it was only a matter of time before the streets and Facebook would close in on her friends. This time now was precious, as she braced for scandal. Desperate times called for desperate measures.

She dialed and waited, rather prayed for an answer. Neko answered.

"What up Tanya, Chloe's not with me."

Neko, already assuming the reason for her, spoke without invitation.

"Do you know where she is?

"Don't know, really don't care. Anyway, there's somebody at my door, holla."

"Wait Neko, I don't know what's going on or if you knew, but there's a picture of you and Jazmine all hugged up posted on Facebook. Doesn't look good Neko."

"Great," Neko responded sarcastically, "thanks for the heads up, bye."

Tanya sat stunned. She replayed her brief conversation with Neko back in her head, outlining the facts. She had told Neko that a pic of him and his girlfriend's best friend was posted online and it didn't look good and he had, upon hearing about it, not given it more than a second thought, on top of that, Jazmine and Chloe were nowhere to be found.

XXIX

Neko was shocked to get a call from Tanya. It seemed like everything was happening at once. Whoever it was at the door was probably pissed or thought he was sneaking a girl out the window or something. What was Tanya talking about, Neko thought. She had said something about a picture of him and Jazmine on Facebook. Where had Chloe run off to? Who the hell was at the door?

He opened the door and found Jazmine. She was standing in one of the stereotypic ways black women stood, hand on her hip, head cocked one way, and she spoke with a smack of her lips, eyes rolling.

"Damn nigga, what took you so long?"

"What are you doing here Jazmine? You can't keep popping up like this, don't look good."

"Well I guess not, after you told Chloe. What happened? You throw a 'wittle temper tantrum because you couldn't get your way? Did you stomp around like a 'wittle boy?"

It was pissing Neko off that she was right, and he still was super-heated from dealing with Chloe. Although Jazmine was the last person he wanted to see, he was relieved to be around somebody he didn't have to maintain appearances for. As if on cue with this thought, he spewed.

"Fuck you."

"Well we could if you weren't suffering from the effects of puppy love Mr. Rose."

If women ever want to know why men spend so much time in the barbershop, this was why. Around certain, well most women, appearances and courtesies had to be maintained. Neko felt he couldn't completely relax around Chloe because she picked at his words, always quick to say, "Who you think you talking to," or, "what does that supposed to mean." Overall, consistently focusing on how things are said as opposed to what's being said. This was nit-picky at best, but still Neko enjoyed being able to take the gloves off. This usually took place at male meeting grounds like barbershops or talking to someone you didn't care for that much, enter Jazmine. Understandably, this went both ways.

"What's the matter playboy, your little girlfriend got your panties in a bunch?"

"Hey, next time don't just pop up at my door or your ass just gone be sitting outside."

"Who said there would be a next time?"

This was going nowhere, Neko thought.

"What do you want anyway?"

"I want to know why you broke our arrangement and what to expect next time I talk to Chloe. Tanya already called me, so I'm assuming she knows, and if your behavior is any type of indicator, the whole hood gone know. I have a reputation to protect."

"OK, home wrecker."

Neko couldn't resist that one.

"Your girl was feeling herself, and besides she got her own skeletons, she was out with her boy Garrett last night. I guess to tell him he might be a daddy, or maybe you knew that."

"No, Chloe's a good girl; she always did her dirt on the low."

"And Tanya called me too, apparently its pictures of me and you on Facebook in a way that would be considered unflattering."

"What, did you post something?"

"Fuck are you talking about, why would I do that?"

"I don't know. I didn't post anything, like I said; I thought we had an arrangement. Maybe your ass should've taken a timeout or something before you decided to become Mr. Joe Truthful and shit. I'd rather be dealing with a picture on Facebook than you running off at the mouth because you mad."

"Hmmm……Let me think, maybe we could've waited a few months until Chloe saw the pudge in your stomach."

Jazmine's look turned cold.

"Oh, you thought I didn't peep that last night, huh? When were you planning on telling me that, or would you rather that had ended up on Facebook too?"

Jazmine just sat there with her head down. They both silently realized they were getting nowhere. Just then Smoke walked in.

"Neko! Yo, Neko! Your door was open and I just wanted to grab…."

Smoke froze when he saw Jazmine. Taking in the scene. Then he displayed one of the dirtiest grins you could ever imagine.

"Well 'lookie, 'lookie at the Facebook celebrities. I'm ready for my close-up Mr. Rose," mimicking Jazmine, half bent over a chair. The cat was definitely out of the bag.

XXX

Chloe walked into her apartment, locking both locks behind her. She was in one of those moods where she preferred nobody in and nobody out. If it was up to her, she was just fine not stepping a foot outside of her apartment anytime in the near future. She had turned her phone on silent, wishing to completely isolate herself from the outside world. Far as she was concerned, she was finished allowing others to dictate her life. And if that meant going it alone with the baby, then so be it. She was quite sure everybody would have something to say or an opinion on what was going on and what she should do. As of now though, the situations that had unfolded in her life over the last two days were about to commit suicide. They would be dead to her because what was the point in having friends and/or lovers if this could be the outcome?

Chloe couldn't figure why she wouldn't be allowed to celebrate the birth of her child with her loved ones. What had she done so wrong that, if karma existed, was coming back to her so hard? She tried to force herself not to feel like these events were her fault but she couldn't. She could do nothing but wonder what she could have done differently. Over the next half hour she tried painstakingly to occupy herself, although this tiny block of time felt like thirty days instead of thirty minutes. She tried to eat, tried to clean, turned on some music, tried to read the bible, prayed, looked at some old photos, cried, and ultimately collapsed on her couch, defeated by the clock, which seemed to not want to move. She sat for a few minutes, before switching on the TV. Players Club was on, fitting Chloe thought. It was on the part where Diamond's cousin sleeps with her man, she actually smiled at this, gesturing to the powers that be that she understood their sense of humor. That was on, which made her think of Jazmine, basketball was on which made her think of Neko, and Soul Plane was on BET, which didn't make her think at all. She cut the TV off.

She couldn't help but wonder about the circumstances of what Neko had said. She was having a hard time believing that Neko would mess around with Jazmine, but why would he lie about something like that? Why would he tell her about it unless he was very upset and really could care less about her feelings? Who does that? She wondered this aloud. These thoughts brought tears with them. She was trying to be strong, but it just wasn't working.

"Chloe!"

"Chloe!"

Someone was yelling her name from outside. She walked to the window knowing it wasn't Neko's voice, thinking how mad she would act if it was, revealing that she secretly hoped it was him. It was Garrett. He staggered around. He looked drunk, as if he hadn't stopped drinking or been to sleep since last night. She picked up her phone, seeing Tanya's missed calls; shrugging it off, still unsure if Tanya was somehow involved. She dialed Garrett while looking out the window. She watched him fumble for his phone like a chain smoker checking every pocket looking for their lighter. He was either drunk or high, either one in itself a shock to her. Either way, he was definitely somewhere else. Finally he grabbed his phone and then struggled a few minutes to simply find the talk button.

"What are you doing Garrett? Do you know these people in my building will call the police on your ass so fast," Chloe laid right into him.

"Chloe I'm sorry about last night," Garrett responded, his speech completely slurred, "let me up."

"Are you fucking kidding me Garrett?"

"I want to have a talk like we used to, you know I'll always be here. Plus we got years in the game."

"No thanks Garrett, you've done enough, and plus you look and sound like you've lost your mind."

Chloe watched him pace the sidewalk. He made demonstrative hand gestures as he spoke. She actually laughed, he looked ridiculous.

"Come on Chloe. I was off my square for one night. I know we're not like that and yes, I've had a little to drink. Help me out here; I don't know who else I could've turned to. Chloe it's killing me how I might have jeopardized our friendship."

He sounded somewhat sincere, but Chloe didn't trust anybody at the moment.

"How about this Garrett, you can go to your car, sleep off the alcohol, I'll call your car in to my building, so you're not towed."

"Oh it's like that?"

"It's like that."

"OK," Garrett said as he walked away, "talk to you later, friend."

Garrett hung up, Chloe simultaneously breathed a sigh of relief and had to admit to herself that that had just been a crazy ass encounter and did a pepper spray check in her purse and made sure her door was locked. After a couple of minutes, she started to relax. Reminding herself that Garrett wasn't crazy, just drunk probably. She walked around looking for the number to call his car in, assuming cooler heads had prevailed and had gone to his car to sleep it off. That's when she got the police knock at the door.

"Chloe!"

OK, it was official. That was Garrett. He had gotten upstairs somehow, and he was fully prepared to act a fool.

"Let me in Chloe! I want to talk to you," Garrett said as he knocked harder and louder.

Chloe in the midst of all this sent a text, responding as she typed.

"Go home Garrett, I'm not letting you in and I'm about two seconds from calling the police."

"On me! Chloe you calling the police on me after everything we've been through?"

He knocked again. Each time he knocked, successively harder. Her door wasn't built for this. She tried to sound calm and stern, but Chloe was really scared to death. All the Jerry Springer and Oprah episodes about crazy ex-boyfriends flashed into her head. She squeezed her eye shut for a moment, praying to God that this and everything else that had happened over the last day and a half had only been a bad dream. No luck. This was real.

"Garrett I'm calling 911," Chloe threatened.

Suddenly, Garrett kicked her door in, startling Chloe. She dropped her phone, visibly shaken up by what was going on.

"Garrett what the fuck is wrong with you, you gone pay for that shit," Chloe screamed, now really pissed, running off shear adrenaline. Garrett's eyes were bloodshot and he looked like he was on whatever.

XXXI

"I'm glad everybody's having such a great time at my expense," Neko said.

Jazmine looked embarrassed but defiant at the same time, if that was at all possible and Smoke looked like he was enjoying a movie as all the drama unfolded.

"My bad bro, but real talk, you got the streets buzzing. Hey 'yo Jaz, so that's what you on? You play hard to get with me, but my boy Neko here can just slide right in huh?"

"Fuck you Smoke, Neko ain't sliding in shit, and you couldn't slide in if it was the electric slide at a family reunion," Jazmine shot back.

Neko had to chuckle at that one, even though he was trying to be serious. Smoke though, true to form, resisted every opportunity to look at the situation with any type of regard.

"I understand completely Jazmine, you only like them if they belong to somebody else, or were the pictures on Facebook an ode to Chloe? Wait! Let me see, would Chloe know or not know that you here at Neko apartment right now? I thought so. Neko you a bad boy."

Smoke ranted on, he was having a field day. Jazmine was turning red. Neko's slight chuckle was turning to a look of concern. This isn't what he wanted. He wasn't interested in Jazmine. He wasn't even sure if he was interested in Chloe, but he loved her, and having all their names dragged through the mud publicly definitely isn't what he wanted. His encounter with Jazmine had been a mistake. Decadence recognized. She had represented Neko getting his way. He was slowly realizing just how big the mess was he had gotten himself into. Ironically, amidst this public relations disaster, he began to relish the idea that Jazmine only wanted one thing. She wasn't the mental cluster that dealing with Chloe was. He knew she wanted more, despite her friendship with Chloe. But she was content moving at the pace Neko set. Control. Funny what gets a man off. She suddenly was "wearing" those jeans in Neko's eyes, and he knew he could have his way.

"Smoke I know you enjoying yourself, but I kind of need to talk to Jazmine privately if you didn't notice."

Smoke caught this hint immediately, but still couldn't let the moment pass that easily.

"Oh, I get it. Wink, wink. OK, Neko. Call me later. Wink, wink."

Jazmine, uncomfortable with how she was being portrayed, only looked the part, actually excited Neko showed initiative at all. Neko walked to the door, non-verbally signaling that Smoke should follow. Jazmine stepped over to his desk, eager to check Facebook for the photos, somewhat intrigued by what all the fuss was about. Neko gave Smoke a pound, ushering him out, as they both watched Jazmine bent over the desk. Smoke bit his fist, illustrating his envy of what Neko was about to have his way with, then miming a hand to his ear, signaling that Neko call him. Neko obliged, shutting the door on him. Then turning to Jazmine, marveled at his conquest. Her ass looked just right, Neko thought. He secretly wondered if women truly knew what they were doing with their movements, if Jazmine knew her body language said "come and get me." He also wondered if she knew that the fact Neko knew she was forbidden was what was driving him right now.

"What the fuck," Jazmine said, squiggling on her toes, "these pics bogus, we must have been outta there."

Neko wasn't listening, just watching.

"Dude bogus for posting these," Jazmine continued before feeling Neko behind her.

"Oh, what's that? What you on Neko?"

She asked this as she slightly stepped back, grinding against him. She wanted him, her slight front, just a formality. He shot his pelvis into her, grabbing her, cupping her breasts.

"Stop," she said, so submissive, might as well have said, 'come get it. Neko had every intention to do just that.

"You want me?" Neko whispered in her ear.

"What you think?"

Jazmine replied, while Neko was cupping his hands on her breasts, pulsating her body into his. Neko turned her around, pushing her head down. She made no attempt to stop him, unbuckling his pants. Before he gave her any help, his pants were coming down, and Jazmine was going to work, neck moving slowly. Neko rested his hands on her head, cocking his head back in triumph. Just then his phone went off. He wasn't going to check it, but secretly he wanted it to be Smoke, just so he could answer say he was busy. Men. It was a text from Chloe.

I know you probably don't care, but Garrett just busted in my apartment. He drunk and I'm scared Neko. Help me please.

Neko shot up. Jazmine thought he was about to come and tried to re-insert. Neko grabbed his genitalia, pulled up his pants, and was halfway out the door before Jazmine could utter, "Neko, what's wrong?"

"Chloe's in trouble," is all she could make out from Neko, because he was already halfway down the stairs.

XXXII

"Why you doing this Chloe?"

Garrett approached Chloe as if she was pulling his strings like a puppet master, as if she was in control. He spoke as if she was the one making him act this way.

"I'm just trying to make things right. I know I messed up. I'm trying to apologize and hopefully see if we can put this behind us."

"First of all, there's no us Garrett, and secondly you could have done all of that over the phone."

Chloe responded, trying to sound calm, but visibly shaken up after Garrett had just kicked her door in. although she was afraid, she was perplexed as to why he had to kick the door in to "talk." She had texted Neko, the last person who might respond at this moment, but the first person she thought to call for help. Garrett continued to approach Chloe slowly, pleading his case with each step.

"Just calm down Chloe. It's me. It's me, Garrett."

Chloe knew who he was but didn't recognize him as she looked in his eyes, which were still completely bloodshot.

"I'm bout to call the police Garrett, this ain't cool."

Chloe spoke sternly, but wasn't trying to provoke Garrett. She doubted if he was much for threats right now. It dawned on her that she wasn't hoping for a favorable outcome of the ordeal just for her, but for her baby as well. This renewed her resolve to navigate through this issue.

"Garrett, let's just forget this ever happened. I'll take care of the door; you go home so I can get a police report. I'll say it was a break-in. No harm, no foul. Then let's just sort everything out tomorrow. OK, hun?"

She spoke these words smooth and deliberated, as if she was teaching a five year old how to tie their shoes. She nodded as she spoke, looking Garrett right in the eye, smiling as Garrett nodded too. Garrett stopped approaching her, processing the information, seeming to agree. Things looked well until Garrett noticed her holding on to her pepper spray behind her back. Chloe's idea for a peaceful resolution was fading fast.

"You gone spray me with that Chloe?"

Garrett spoke, motioning to the pepper spray behind her back.

"Is that what we on?"

As if snapping out of a trance, Garrett lunged at Chloe. He grabbed her arm, trying to shake the pepper spray free. Chloe screamed, "Garrett, let go of me, help!" Garrett wrestled the pepper spray free, and Chloe smacked him across the face with her free hand. At that instant, Garrett staggered backwards. He touched his face with a look of disbelief. Chloe watched as this look of bewilderment was evaporating into rage. Garrett lunged at Chloe, muffing her. Knocking her to the floor, into a stool and crashing onto the floor. She hit her head with a thud, and then quickly staggered to her feet. Garrett looked as if he couldn't believe what he had just done.

"I'm sorry Chloe. Are you OK? I didn't mean to hurt you?"

They both sat there, face to face, about to five feet apart. Chloe eyes were now bloodshot to match Garrett's. He carried a look of a father after spanking a child, knowing he may have just gone too far. Chloe was trying to hold back the tears, refusing to give Garrett the satisfaction of knowing how scared and vulnerable she felt.

"What you want me to do Chloe? I'll do it. I'm sorry. I didn't mean to. You know that right?"

Garrett was rambling. It seemed as if he had regained his senses and was starting to understand how bad this all looked. A door kicked in, and a woman he had just assaulted. He was no police officer, but that sounded a lot like criminal trespassing and domestic battery. These thoughts he was having also indicated he was sobering up quick.

"You alright Chloe?"

Garrett continued. Chloe had a glazed look on her face. She was angry at being afraid. The past two days flashed in front of her. She couldn't understand why all this was happening to her, but she was sick and tired of being afraid. All types of emotions began to well up inside her. But defiance was emerging as the dominant one.

"Get the hell out of my house Garrett!"

Chloe said this without looking at Garrett. She was staring off into another direction. She spoke in a tone of impending danger for those who didn't heed her words. Like a mother speaking to a child in public, letting him or her know "it's on" when we get home.

"Get the hell out of my house now Garrett!"

Garrett bounced back, making clear he heard her.

"Alright, if you are sure you're OK, I'm gone."

Chloe shot him a look that would have given Satan pause. Garrett left much quieter than he had come. Chloe slumped down and cried. She was scared, yes. But now she cried because of what she might have done. She cried because she was afraid of herself and for anybody who got in the way of her and her child.

"Chloe."

Chloe heard her name, and devilishly wished it was Garrett again.

"I swear to God Garrett, if you don't leave me alone."

Neko appeared at her door, surveying the scene. He stepped towards Chloe. She noticeably tensed up.

"Chloe, you OK? What happened?"

Neko was trying to help, but to Chloe it all sounded the same.

"Leave me alone," was all she could muster.

CHLOE: in her own words...

If we knew then what we know now...would we still love...would we still try...hurt so bad...can we still lie...can we say its ok when we still cry...sweet lover tell me why'd you steal my heart...I need it back its still mine...chose to share it with you...chose to hug and kiss you...what were you thinking...what could I have done...so blind, from whom do you get your advice...is this ok in your eyes...god bless, to make it this far has taken a short memory...ignoring countless people who've asked what's gotten into me...but now I'm sitting here broken...my tears could fill an ocean...requests to respect my love...like letters that have never been opened...and only now you feel sorry...how I hate your dirty game...how I hate how I react...at every mention of your name...cuz I give you your power so I'm half to blame...but one of us will move on and one of us will never be the same...scared to be around you...you'll probably do it again...but I can't stand to be without you...ain't that a crying shame...thinking to myself how much will it take...for me to get the point...for me to walk away...or stay...why should I leave when you're already gone...why should I take responsibility when the responsibilities yours...you caused all this you shut the doors...you made me think it was over...then you wanted more...you you you!...its always been you...sometimes I say its not but we know the truth...sometimes we've stopped...but I willed us to move...and sometimes we win...sometimes we lose...

CHLOE BRYANT

XXXIII

Neko watched Chloe and couldn't help but feel ashamed.

"Chloe let me help. It's still me, what happened?"

Chloe sat, knees bent, arms wrapped around them, shaking like she was a crack feen in search of a hit. Neko only saw the mother of his child, helpless. He began to approach her, but she motioned for him to stop. She sobbed and did nothing but rock herself back and forth.

"Chloe, whatever happened, we'll get through it, together."

Neko said this sincerely. An hour ago, Chloe would have melted at the sound of these words, but now they were words.

"I can't do this Neko. I'm sorry, but I just can't," Chloe finally spoke.

"Can't do what? What are you talking about Chloe? Just tell me what happened; let's focus on making sure your OK."

"You don't get it Neko. That's just it; I can't have myself mixed up in these ridiculous situations. Crazed ex-boyfriends busting in my house, you sleeping with so called best friends, and not to mention the roller coaster which is us. I'm going to be a mom Neko. I'm going to be somebody's mom. There's just no time for this type of shit. Just can't do it anymore."

Chloe was speaking to Neko, but was staring off into space. She spoke purposefully, and she knew he heard her. It was funny to her in a cynical, morbid type of way how yelling, pleading, and begging, wasn't necessary to get through to Neko. She was talking directly to him and she knew she was getting through. Neko stood in the middle of her kitchen as if on an island surrounded by shark infested waters, where one step meant imminent doom. It seemed as if he was completely aware how sensitive this moment was and how important it was to tread carefully. This idea told him that "I'm sorry's," or "what about the things you did's" weren't going to get them anywhere. This wasn't a blame game. Chloe wasn't playing, it was an end game, make no mistake. Neko wasn't himself 100% with him and Chloe going forward, he was still up in the air about the baby "thing," but couldn't have foreseen things going this way. Neko felt further shame that if this was the end, he was upset he didn't get to end it. Chloe was right. They had made a complete mess of what they had. Neko slowly began to realize the gravity of the situation. It was sinking in slowly that a baby was coming. You couldn't explain to the child some of the issues its parents were facing and have it understand.

This revelation hit Neko like a ton of bricks, so much so that his knees buckled. His eyes were watering up. He was losing Chloe and watching it happen. What would this mean for the child? Why had it taken so much bullshit to happen to understand what was really important? Why was his acceptance of life as he had made it costing him Chloe? Neko clearly understood where Chloe was coming from. She hadn't moved a muscle. It was as if she knew she had just dropped a bomb and was allowing for everything to sink in. Neko wasn't sure what to do. He was upset, sad, mad, frustrated, and concerned all at the same time. He decided to do what he thought Chloe would. He spoke slowly.

"Chloe, I'm not sure what the future holds but right now I need to make sure you're OK."

"I'm OK, Neko."

Her reply favored on the side of sarcasm to him. He couldn't shake the feeling that she was brushing him off. He tried to address the topic again, but this time took a different approach.

"Chloe you can't tell me you are OK with the door busted open and you're on the kitchen floor, balled up crying. I understand your feelings but if we're to be concerned about what's really important, we need to make sure you're OK."

"Neko, I'm fine. I think I just need…."

"Stop telling me your fine Chloe, you didn't have a nightmare you can just wake up from! Don't text me in distress and then act like it didn't happen. Don't tell me you're OK when I'm looking at what I'm looking at. We're all going to do what we have to do, I get that, I really do. But don't for one second ask me not to care."

Neko's words came out choppy, he was obviously choked up. He never understood why he got so much resistance when he said and did what Chloe had wanted him to do. He was growing more frustrated by the moment. Chloe was detached. Neko was losing his bearings.

"What do you want me to do," Neko lost it; he crumbled to his knees, tears welling up and beginning to fall.

"I only wanted you, always just you. Nothing I did was ever to make you feel different than that. I always wanted to be the one to make your life OK."

Chloe cut him off.

"Neko, I'm OK, I just need some time."

Neko felt defeated and wanted less to bother Chloe if she just wanted him gone, which seemed apparent. They both sat there in silence, staring off into space.

XXXIV

This hadn't been the first time Neko and Chloe had decided on eithers request to "go on hiatus." Only six months into their relationship their wills had been tested. It was that point in time all couples go through, no matter what their maturation point may be. Neko was catching heat from Smoke and his boys about all the time he was spending with Chloe. Chloe was questioning if she was really over Garrett. While these thoughts played out on the subconscious level, it caused for tension on the surface. If it's true you wear your heart on your sleeve, Neko and Chloe could illustrate. These thoughts they carried produced insecurities that led to senseless spats with his boys in his ear, Neko would give off a vibe that suggested Chloe was smothering him; this would in turn cause Chloe to question her seriousness with Neko, at a time where she was struggling with the idea of a serious relationship because of Garrett. Deep down the two really loved each other, but a lot of times love is tested through fire. Moments like these where there's a fork in the road, and your faith in one another is what has to propel a relationship forward because there isn't enough substance there yet. It's hard admittedly though, to step out on a ledge with your heart. And things are even harder when you're not sure of the intentions of your significant other. Neko knew he loved Chloe very early. Chloe admittedly, needed more time. The two explained this to one another and Neko put faith in Chloe based solely on the idea that at least Chloe was willing to go forward to see what happens. These things are easy in the beginning, when young couples are in "La La Land," but as the dust settles and your significant other isn't a little secret anymore but actually a significant part of life, honest assessments need to be made.

But usually out of fear these conversations are avoided because no one wants to hear the other side of the story where feelings aren't reciprocated. Chloe did have the heart to tell Neko she had doubts, but not the heart to declare exactly what side of the fence she was on. Neko didn't really care what his friends or anybody thought about his involvement with Chloe. He hadn't even considered stepping out on her. He also didn't have the heart to put these thoughts into action, choosing instead to adhere to the status quo which mandated he shy away from serious relationship status when they hadn't even gotten serious yet. All this confusion between the two and if you asked either Neko or Chloe to point out there discrepancies with the other, they'd be hard-pressed. They both wondered aloud, looking back, why if the love was so obvious, then why were so many constant miscommunications or hurdles? Unbeknownst to them, each "mini-battle" they fought was another notch in their respective belt. Strength in one another was being built each time they didn't walk away, but right now they were facing their toughest obstacle to date, and both doubted if they would ever see the light of day or if the love was strong enough to carry them this time.

XXXV

Chloe awoke the next morning after well needed good night's rest. She had experienced one of those good sleeps that made her wonder if everything she'd experienced over the last couple of days had been nothing more than a bad dream. But quickly realizing that Trix were for kids, she sat up and immediately began to assess how to handle what she felt she had to do. First and foremost, she felt the welfare of her unborn child should take precedent. As she scanned over the other issues in her life that may demand her attention, she began to realize how much work she would have to do to make things right with people that had wronged her. Neko had been a complete and utter jerk about the baby and her feelings about it. She had tried to communicate with him about it and he had been stand-offish and rude. Chloe in turn confided in her ex-boyfriend Garrett, which had admittedly been a horrible move as he was only out for the one thing men are only out for. These events led to the Jerry Springer-esque revelation that Neko and Chloe's best friend Jazmine had been sleeping around or at least that's what had been rumored. Chloe had yet to talk to Jazmine. That one really stung. Chloe knew something was to it, considering Jazmine hadn't jumped up to clear her name. Chloe wondered how she should even address this, or if she should address it all. To her it had become clear that while the company she kept may not be all evil, there always seemed to be some type of commotion. Chloe wondered if this drama would be conducive to trying to properly raise a child. She was hesitant in these thoughts though; tip-toeing purposefully around the fact that she was contemplating life without Neko, the father. Chloe felt like she was stuck at the point that a lot of young mother's in today's society find themselves in. That point where she would have to take on the role of bad guy because nobody else involved seemed to notice the child is more important.

Chloe had heard stories about young women painted as villains because they had created distance between themselves and their "baby-daddies," for the sake of the child. Why was that the case? Why was the mother crucified if the father wanted to sleep around and basically do the family thing only when it worked out for him? Fathers today are generally given chance after chance to assume their position as head of household. Typically though, these fathers mire themselves in immaturity, only to receive undeserved pats on the back for simply showing up at birthday parties. This made absolutely no sense to Chloe, she questioned if it ever should.

She walked into her kitchen, instantly reminding herself of Garrett's exploit the day before, which had left her doorless and having to take the day off from work to wait around for the landlord to come fix it. If you could look up in the dictionary and find how to get yourself cancelled in Chloe's social world, Garrett would be the poster boy. She had no intentions of ever having anything to do with him again, and she was still debating if she should have some of the guys she knew from her old neighborhood pay him a visit, because he definitely had earned one. Chloe still felt terrible about letting herself almost slip with Garrett.

Every time she thought about what damage it could create for her and Neko, she reminded herself about the matter with Jazmine. Word was there were pics on Facebook of the two. Plus, Neko had admitted, although in anger, that something had went down. All of this was hard to swallow. Every time Chloe thought about this she got sick to her stomach. She wanted so badly to get "ghetto" and call that bitch out. But something inside her, regarding this situation, and the others over the past weekend, was telling her to fall back. If the people in her life she once considered close wanted to keep up this type of mess, go ahead. They would just have to do it without her.

In reality, there was no time for drama. Chloe felt comfort in the independence she was affirming in these thoughts. She walked in her bathroom, looked in the mirror and did something she hadn't remembered doing the last couple of days, she smiled. She made a funny face, laughing at herself as she pantomimed wiping dirt off her shoulder. She then decided that today would be a Chloe day. Why not? She was off work and could use some "me" time to get her mind re-focused on what was most important, her baby. She rubbed her stomach, sighing in relief. Taking solace in the fact that at least one thing would turn out good from the situations she was facing.

XXXVI

"Neko Rose you put this baby in, help me get out now!"

Neko awoke from his dream in a cold seat. He sat up and allowed reality to sink in. he had dreamed that he received a text saying it was time for the baby to come. He then rushed to the hospital only to find that both Chloe and Jazmine were in the same room, both delivering his children. In the dream they both had cried out for his attention during labor and he had sat frozen not knowing what to do. Neko was starting to realize this might not have been just a dream. There was a strong possibility Jazmine had gotten pregnant and the baby could be his. He had no idea where he and Chloe stood. Yesterday when he left Chloe's apartment, she had looked at Neko in a way he had never seen. He couldn't get that stare out of his mind. He was having trouble because Chloe had looked at him with such pain and anger but also what he felt when she looked at him was a sense of Chloe having had enough. Chloe had looked depleted.

Neko knew that he had a lot do with all the stress she was under, before you even got to the baby. Neko also knew there would be no way for anyone to examine what he was going through. Neko wasn't out for sympathy and was fully aware that the concerns of the baby took precedence. Neko had done the unthinkable. He had slept with Chloe's best friend. As he reminded himself of this and the ultra-inconsiderate way he had gone about telling Chloe. If she hadn't already been privy to the photos allegedly floating around Facebook, he knew he couldn't blame Chloe for how she had or would react. He was unsure what she knew outside of what he had said. He didn't know if she had talked to Jazmine. If Jazmine's demeanor was any indicator to how she might react to a talk with Chloe, things wouldn't go well. Jazmine was giving off a vibe that suggested to Neko that she really didn't care what Chloe thought and that it was every woman for themselves when it came to Neko. Neko had no interest in Jazmine and felt terrible how he had antagonized this situation by even sleeping with Jazmine. He had been a brat. He had risked what he had at home for a little attention, a phat ass, and a pretty face. The only thing he liked about Jazmine is that he got his way. He also knew that this was superficial and that he and Jazmine would never amount to what he and Chloe had taken years to build. He knew how the story would be told though as well.

Neko would be portrayed as this terrible man who had taken advantage of two girls who had been friends since they were children. He had divided them, impregnating both and for reasons unknown, wasn't with either one of them. No one would care who Neko really was, let alone take the time to find out. He could envision the looks he would get even after introducing himself and telling his kids, and how he would be frowned upon. How if he ever tried to say this treatment was unfair, he would be labeled as a man who "didn't get it." But he did, Neko knew very well that these girls had him by the balls. They would dictate his life for the next twenty years or so. He would have no identity outside of "baby-daddy." Neko was fully aware of the same being true for women, that their lives too would be dictated by the children. These girls would earn their perception by what they did. Neko would earn his by their recommendation. Neko had been privy to many situations where men had made every attempt to do right by their children, but if the women found any fault, be it merited or not, the men fit whatever description they were given. If they say men are deadbeats, they're deadbeats. If a man gives his all, and he and the mother are not together, the input will never equate. The truth is once that decision is made, the mother will do more and the father will have no choice but to stand idly by and facilitate leaving himself in a lose-lose situation and at the mercy of his "baby-momma."

These same politics are what led Neko astray in the first place. Dealing with Chloe, she had taken for granted that he had feelings too. Maybe this had happened because men aren't expected to have them. Most women, Neko thought, seem to feel if they have sex when a man wants, this qualifies them to say they "take care of home." In most cases they don't even get the sex part right, let alone begin to comprehend what it means to "take care of home." Men are simple creatures. Neko felt women do nothing more than try to make two plus two equal five, instead of accepting the true math. When a man tries to correct his woman, she becomes defensive or shuts down. Neko had heard an old saying once that he felt summed things up pretty well. If a man's asked what she thinks of something, no matter what it is, he'll say if he likes it or not. A woman on the other hand, will say, "I don't know, what you think?" This leaves the man on the ledge. This removes the woman from a position of responsibility. Perching her right where she wants, in a position of critique.

Neko felt he would never be Neko again. He got up and walked around half asleep getting himself dressed. There was one bright side to this unfortunate paradigm. If all women thought we thought about was sports and video games, Neko was prepared to fully feed into that idea 100%. Complete with a huge Tupperware bowl full of Fruit Loops, he sat on his couch, and prepared himself not to move, for a while.

XXXVII

Jazmine was debating on how she should tell Neko she was pregnant. She was leaving the doctor's office. Ironically the same doctor's office Chloe had just left two days prior. As she thought to herself, she wondered which mode of communication would be most effective. She couldn't help but wonder what his response would be. Would he be upset, happy, sad, or mad? She understood completely what kind of line she was walking and understood to get what she wanted; she would have to be careful. Jazmine considered herself well-seasoned when it came to men. She felt they were weak and of the flesh. She wanted Neko. She didn't consider him wanting her back a matter of heart but rather a matter of survival. She would simply make sure she was the last woman standing.

Although it pained her thinking about the ramifications this would have on her and Chloe's relationship, she couldn't help but stick to her motto of "everything's fair in love in war." Jazmine felt, unlike Chloe, that Neko was a suitable mate. Intelligent, attractive brothers of character didn't grow on trees and Jazmine had secretly grown tired of watching Chloe squander her relationship with Neko by constantly picking at him about nonsense and constantly being so indecisive with her feelings. Jazmine reasoned that if Chloe didn't have sense enough to snatch Neko up, she would. Hopefully, Chloe would understand, as Jazmine had every intention of explaining this to Chloe. Jazmine was aware that Chloe might accuse her of being phony considering that she had never been an ally of Neko's, always advising Chloe to dump him Jazmine planned to only clarify that if Chloe wasn't sure if she wanted Neko or not, she should've moved on. Jazmine figured matters of the heart worked how she was playing things. You see what you want and you go get it, especially as a woman. Your success was tied to what you would be willing to endure. Did it bother her that Neko took a rain check on her yesterday to go to Chloe's right before they were about to have sex? Of course it did but Jazmine also knew Chloe and with so many issues in play, she was going to do nothing but be overly dramatic about her feelings, which would eventually wear Neko down anyway. So in essence, Jazmine was banking on Chloe leading Neko right to her. All she would have to do is make herself available.

She understood the weird ways men worked and how hot and cold Neko would run. She also knew men were creatures of habit. Once Neko understood "it" was his and that he would encounter little resistance or nagging, coupled with how flattered he would be that a chick of Jazmine's status was jocking him, things would take shape all on their own. Jazmine had long tried to school Chloe to this way of thinking but Chloe, in Jazmine's eyes, tended to over think things. Chloe was what Jazmine would call a hopeless romantic. She was too concerned with how things should be as opposed to accepting how they are. Jazmine felt she always had a leg up on most women because she simply understood you can't make something into something it's not. Most people didn't get that idea when Jazmine would try to explain it to them, but it made perfect sense to her. So while most women chased their happiness, Jazmine preferred to create hers.

She hoped with how well Chloe knew her she would just understand, although Jazmine would confess this was nothing more than wishful thinking. She was, in fact, by her actions proclaiming that her relationship with Chloe was expendable. Point blank. She was prepared for the ridicule she would face from all over the place. She would lose Chloe and possibly Tanya. She would be labeled as a hoe or home wrecker. She would have to accept things. Jazmine felt she had a better grasp on the big picture than most because while people would be busy name calling, she would also have the man she wanted. A kid, which she wanted, and right on pace with what plans she had made for her life. Jazmine didn't worry herself with how she got from point A to B; she just concerned herself with getting there at all. So, in Jazmine's eyes, everybody could fall back, because all Jazmine was about, was winning.

While on the surface people ridiculed her, she knew people secretly envied her. She would do things other women wouldn't, so it only made sense that she would get to enjoy things other women didn't. Feelings aside, she decided to simply text Neko. No need for a "feelings parade." Just as long as he knew. If he wanted to speak further, he could come to her. She would make herself available. She glanced in her rear-view mirror, thinking to herself how most nigga's could take lessons from her on how to hustle and get what they want. At a red light, she texted Neko.

I'm pregnant. It's yours.

That was all she wrote. Let the games begin she thought.

XXXVIII

Chloe sat on her couch watching reruns of the Kardashians. She had taken a liking to Kourtney, who managed to maintain her figure, her relationship, her family, and her glamour. She had given birth to her baby boy and seemingly hadn't skipped a beat. Chloe couldn't help but start to have little closet fantasies about what life might be like. She was trying her hardest not to start favoring a boy over a girl although she did kind of want a boy more. She was picturing herself dressing him in all the latest fashions and the special relationship they would have. If allowed to dream, she would. His name would be King. Chloe would cultivate a relationship with him rooted in love, discipline, and friendship. She would push her son to be great. She envisioned them being like Malik and Tasha Mack on The Game.

As the details always flowed easily for her when the subject came to this, it became obvious to her that she had been waiting for this moment all her life. She checked herself, noticing she may be overdoing it just a bit, considering her pregnancy was only about six weeks in. she was relaxed and taking full advantage of her day off. The men the landlord had sent to fix her door had taken a liking to her and were repairing things all over her kitchen for nothing more than a smile in return. She casually flirted with the fine young brother, but never went too far, as Chloe was starting to feel like soon she was going to be somebody's mother. Her focus, again a bit premature, was starting to focus on how she would raise a child. Even as she conversed with the young man, she thought about his parents and how his upbringing had been. Little did he know the smiles he got out of her were smiles resulting from a whole separate side conversation she was having in her head. So when she heard her brand new door swing open, she assumed it was the young handy man returning from lunch. She was wrong.

"Chloe Bryant, what is your problem? Are we not returning phone calls? And what happened to our kitchen door? And why are we not at work? We got some explaining to do Ms. Bryant."

Tanya, without announcing herself, had come in, and seemed to be in full force. Chloe had somehow forgotten all of this as she cocooned herself to her couch. She still was unsure what Tanya knew and what part she played in all this. Her skepticism was getting the better of her, but she couldn't get around how happy she was to see Tanya. Tanya had always been the most even of anybody she knew and regardless of her involvement Tanya would be up front and honest. As usual her demeanor would be sprinkled with hints of optimism. Tanya was like a "pick me up" in a bottle.

"I'm sorry girl; it's been a rough last couple of days."

Chloe responded but was sure to stay vague until she figured out exactly what Tanya knew.

"I've heard," Tanya responded, "you've turned into a ghetto celebrity. What's going on, you and Jaz sharing Neko now? Its pictures all over Facebook that would say so. Did you lend him out or what? And what exactly happened to your kitchen door? You'n knock the heifer out did you?"

Judging from her comments, it seemed as if Tanya knew about as much as Chloe did. This made her feel a bit more comfortable. She dropped her guard, and went over her activities of the last couple of days. Tanya sat listening, mouth dropped, as if she couldn't believe what she was hearing. Chloe explained her talk with Neko, her night with Garrett, what Neko had said about Jazmine, and then how Garrett had seemingly lost his mind.

"Have you talked to anybody? Why didn't you call me? What the hell is wrong with Jazmine?"

Tanya could do nothing but mutter questions, as it was apparent she was still trying to make sense of everything. Chloe went on, nodding her head as she spoke as if to confirm to Tanya that what she was saying, however unbelievable, had actually happened. Tanya's phone rang.

"Speaking of the devil. Guess both you heifer's are deciding to come out of hiding today."

From the response, Chloe knew it was Jazmine. Chloe watched her as she spoke, trying to convince herself she didn't care what they were talking about, but still trying to pick apart what they were talking about.

"Well hello Ms. Busy-body."

"Uhh Huh, I've heard."

"I'm on my lunch break."

"That's fine, but I'm at Chloe's."

"OK."

Tanya hung up her phone and looked over as if her phone call had been invisible. She seemed not to notice how Chloe was waiting for her say something. After she kind of noticed what Chloe's expression was saying, she did.

"Jazmine's on her way over, guess we gone get to the bottom of this."

XXXIX

Neko was trying to focus on the game of NBA 2K12 he was playing, but after a couple of hours, his attempt to his escape his reality through visual stimuli was starting to flat out not work. This was also apparent in the fact the computer was kicking his ass. He wondered what Chloe was doing right now and if she was alright. She hadn't told him and had been super adamant about not wanting to speak with him. Neko wanted to put things with Chloe in the past, but even he knew Chloe was in his life to stay. Because with a baby coming and her intent to keep it, Neko felt he might as well get used to the idea of having Chloe and the child around.

He wondered if he was being selfish though by his thoughts on how to approach Chloe about making things more comfortable for him. Neko was trying to be an adult about this situation. By the way Chloe had acted recently, there was a strong possibility him and Chloe might not make it. Not trying to be a jerk about it, but if Chloe wanted to be done, Neko wanted things to be clear. He wanted no parts of the confusion that comes with babies from parents who aren't together. He felt though that that shouldn't stop him from helping Chloe any way he could, and truly being there for his child. Drama could be avoided Neko thought. Besides, Chloe and his child were what Neko loved the most in this world anyway. He would do anything for them, even if Chloe might have a hard time believing this.

Neko's phone rang; it was a number he didn't recognize. He hesitated a bit before answering.

"Hello?"

"Yes, this is Dr. Sharpley. I was looking for Neko Rose?"

"This is he doctor, how can I help you?"

"I believe we met Saturday when you were in with a Ms. Chloe Bryant."

"Yes, that was me."

"Oh, OK. I'm really sorry to bother you, but I saw a patient this morning who listed you as the person she believed to be the father of the baby she was carrying. I'm not trying to pry, but I wanted to give you a heads up just in case in any event. You seemed like a young brother who had his stuff together. And for every young woman I see who's in a bad situation, there's usually a young man in an equally bad situation, you catch my drift?"

Neko felt embarrassed. He wondered if the doctor had also called Chloe. As if reading Neko's mind, the doctor continued.

"I hadn't spoken with Ms. Bryant; this is as far as I go with these types of things. This was nothing more than a head's up. I hope that things work out for all parties involved. I assume you know who I am speaking of, that can get tricky as I can't divulge the identity."

"Yes doctor, I think I do."

"Good, because legally, I couldn't tell you if I wanted to. Take care Mr. Rose, take care."

The doctor hung up before Neko could thank him. Neko had almost forced himself to think Jazmine couldn't be pregnant, at least by him anyways. He had figured if he kind of avoided it or remained in a state of denial, maybe the situation would go away. This would not be the case. Neko was stating to feel like the weight of the world was on his shoulders. Not only was Chloe pregnant, but Jazmine as well. He wondered if maybe it wasn't his. He didn't know about the sexual exploits of Jazmine. Did she sleep around?

He foresaw the road ahead filled with DNA tests, paternity issues, and child support. No matter if he pursued this or not, this was going to be something he would have to deal with. He felt his chances of ever being with Chloe also slipping away. Not only had he slept with her best friend, but he had gotten her pregnant as well. At that moment he got a text from Jazmine.

I'm pregnant, it's yours.

How nice of her, Neko thought.

XL

"You did not just tell Jazmine to come over here!"

Chloe had barely let the words roll of the tongue of Tanya. Chloe couldn't believe that Tanya had decided on her own to bring things to a head. Chloe didn't know what to think. She wondered if she should be angry, or stand offish. She also wondered what Jazmine's attitude would be. The women had been friends since they were little girls. At this point, Chloe didn't even know what had been done. In the back of her mind she secretly hoped Neko had said what he said out of spite. Then again, there were the pictures on Facebook that Chloe hadn't seen that according to Tanya were causing quite a stir.

"Look Chloe, I don't care what you and her got going on, but we've known each other too long to let a nigga come between us, even if it is Neko. So even if I gotta force ya'll, we gone get some answers today."

Tanya was adamant in what she wanted to see happen and her demeanor suggested that no one get in her way. This had always been Tanya's rule within the group, and right now Chloe felt comforted by it. Her protest about dealing with Jazmine right now was nothing more than a façade. Deep down she knew that Tanya was right, and that her and Jazmine had to get on the same page as far as what was going on.

"Hello?"

Jazmine announced herself as she strode past the work station that had become Chloe's kitchen. She entered the living room, gave a nod to Chloe and then spoke to Tanya.

"What you doing off work, you doing your three hour lunch break thing?"

This was an obvious attempt at humor by Jazmine. This let Chloe know for a fact that something was definitely up. Jazmine was never easily rattled, nor was she one to sugar coat things. She either had something to hide or nothing to hide at all. Again Chloe was unsure. The tension in the room could have suffocated the three girls as they sat momentarily in silence.

"Hey Chloe, what happened in your kitchen and why aren't you at work?"

Jazmine spoke at last. Chloe didn't know this to be an insult or not. But before she could gain her bearing, she did what she was thinking but not what she had wanted to do.

"Are you fucking Neko?"

The words rolled of Chloe's tongue matter-of-factly. Tanya's mouth dropped. Although Tanya had been gung ho about getting answers, even she was surprised at Chloe's more direct approach. Jazmine, as well, looked as if she was taken aback by Chloe's question. By her response, she evidently hadn't come to spar. For a moment, Jazmine looked almost hurt. Chloe saw this and was beginning to think on how to clean things up. As she pondered, Jazmine's expression changed. If she had been communicating non-verbally, you would have witnessed her look of concern erode into a look of "Ok, let's do it then if that's how you want to play it." She tensed up a bit, as if she knew she was about to cross a point of no return.

"Yup," was all that came out of Jazmine's mouth.

If Chloe's question had dropped Tanya's jaw, she might faint at this point. Jazmine and Chloe participated in a virtual stand-off. Both were unwilling to move an inch. Chloe was in a position where she wanted to do a number of different things, with her mindset being on if she should lunge at Jazmine. She still was trying to edge on the side of caution, conceding the benefit of the doubt, understanding that she had created this atmosphere by her aggressive language earlier. She waited for Jazmine to speak again. Deciding that Jazmine would be allowed to determine how things went from here.

"Oh wait," Jazmine reached into her purse, retrieving her phone, "let's have Neko explain."

Jazmine put her phone on speaker.

"Hey boo, I'm here with Chloe and Tanya. Looks like Chloe wanna know if we're fucking. Yes, fucking. I think that's the term she used."

Chloe was losing the battle of trying to stay calm. She couldn't believe this was happening. She had never been gullible, but at the same time, she didn't have a prescribed protocol for instances like this. She felt her emotions leaning towards survival. Her or Jazmine. She was on full alert, but captivated at the same time. It was almost as if she was watching the moments unfold on television. Like a viewer completely taken in by what was being shown, she too sat transfixed waiting for Neko's reply.

XLI

"The fuck are you on Jazmine?"

Neko's tone was firm and unwavering without being ignorant.

"Chloe!"

"Chloe!"

Neko dropped this attitude as he screamed out for Chloe.

"Hmmm….silence is agreeance in my book Neko."

Jazmine spoke as if trying to bait Neko into this sparring match. Chloe and Tanya sat in utter disbelief. Although Neko wasn't giving in completely to what Jazmine was trying to do, it remained obvious that there was evidence of a relationship, in whatever form. Neko and Jazmine spoke to each other definitely as if they knew something that everybody else didn't. Chloe heard Neko calling her name. To her they were cries for help. She had anger building for Jazmine but at the same time, she wanted to ball up and cry. The moment was definitely surreal. Everyone involved would admit though that Jazmine was pulling the strings. She had Neko obviously wanting to avoid saying the truth. Tanya's years of mediating from the middle were useless as she sat, paralyzed as she faced the fact she knew very little about these people she thought she knew. Chloe, who had protected both Neko and Jazmine from her real life belief that you should watch the company you keep, had no idea how to reach out to Neko or if she sould simply try to punch Jazmine, or better yet vice versa.

"Neko, is it true?"

Chloe, aware that she was probably playing into Jazmine's little game, still couldn't resist this to chance to ask Neko directly.

"Chloe, I'm sorry but trust me it's not what it sounds like. Let me explain."

Neko mouthed these words and for the first time started to realize how much he cared for Chloe. It was as if something in him couldn't rest until he at least got to say his peace, if only to make sure she knew the truth. Unfortunately, Jazmine was on the same thing.

"Do you think we should tell her the rest of our good news Neko?"

If this was a heavyweight fight, Jazmine was going for the knockout blow.

"Oh yes, there's more."

Jazmine was speaking in a tone that suggested she was talking to an older sibling, baiting them into a battle they couldn't win, knowing too well how the parents would react.

"Jazmine, if you have any respect for me and Chloe and what we're going through, you'll understand that this is something I want to tell her on my own."

Neko took the high road, leaving the low road to Jazmine and Jazmine alone.

"No Neko, if you had any respect for what you and Chloe were going through, we wouldn't be tap dancing around telling her I'm pregnant also, and also by you!"

The words cut like a knife. If there was a public opinion poll on this, Neko just lost a lot of points.

"No Neko, please tell me you didn't."

Tanya didn't realize she was speaking out loud. She covered her mouth knowing how important it was to not pass judgment until everyone knew the whole story. As optimistic as she was, it was apparent that Neko had a slim to none chance of being able to rationalize his careless and selfish actions. Meanwhile, Chloe couldn't hold it any longer, she wept. Neko, hearing her sobs, called out to her.

"Chloe!"

"Chloe?"

"Neko, maybe you should let this one breathe," Tanya muttered.

All that was audible was Chloe's sobs. Neko hung up. He could think of nothing but Chloe's pain. Right then he decided to face this, ignoring Tanya's advice. He left immediately for Chloe's.

XLII

"Chloe? Are you alright?"

Tanya mouthed these words to Chloe. Chloe again sat motionless. She was more upset with herself than anyone else. Not more than 24 hours ago she sat in this same state. Her world turned upside down by people she had extended trust to. Now here she sat again, in her own home, amongst antagonists and those she was uncertain had her best interest in mind. She knew her continued silence would be taken as a breakdown. But she wondered why she should be in such a hurry to talk them. Besides, what good would talk do at this point? In Chloe's eyes, she was receiving confirmation on what she had been thinking to herself all along. It's her and her baby. These extra distractions were nothing more than extra chances to get caught up in some bullshit. Right now she saw this situation and collection of people in her home as nothing more than land mines, prepared to go off, with only one false step. What was there to gain? Tanya was going to try and be somebody's mama or social worker or psychiatrist or whatever it is that she always did. Jazmine was operating right now without Chloe's foot up her ass by the grace of God, Chloe thought. These were negative thoughts Chloe was thinking, but she reasoned that confirmed by the actions at hand that we live in a negative world. As of now, Chloe was content with simply waiting them out. Eventually they would leave. Sarcastically she thought, "It's not like they're true friends anyway. It's not like these people have her best interest at heart."

So she sat, ignoring their questions and overtures to join them. They all wanted to know how she felt. Why should she give them the pleasure? In what world would any of them be able to understand what she was going through? Chloe wasn't claiming to have the monopoly on pain and cold shoulders, but realistically what was to be gained by nurturing these relationships any further? The more Chloe thought about this, the more she questioned her reason for being there.

"Chloe?"

Questions to gauge her well-being at this point continued. She continued to ignore, more interested in the dialogue she was having within herself.

"Niggas."

Tanya tried the "good ol' men are the root of evil" tactic. No dice. Followed by Jazmine's, "girl, I'm sorry you have to go through this, if I could go back and change this I would." Even Tanya had to giggle at that because Stevie Wonder could see Jazmine was empty of sincerity. Chloe got up and left the room, it could definitely stand to go on without her. And it did, once Chloe cleared her bedroom, Tanya went right in.

"Heifer you gotta lotta nerve. What were you thinking?"

"Spare me Tanya; I've provided more clarity to Neko and Chloe's relationship than those two ever could have in the three years. Plus, the next three."

"Jazmine, you ain't God. So what, things aren't progressing fast enough for you in Neko and Chloe's relationship, that you feel getting knocked up by Neko is going to make things better?"

"I hear you Tanya. But don't tell me for one minute you were confident those two were on a path to figuring things out. They were the most 'in love'ingest but I still don't know what we're going to do' couple I've ever seen. At least now everyone knows where they stand."

"So what, you feel they should be thanking you? You and Chloe have been friends since you two still wet the bed and this is your idea of best friend intervention?"

"For what's going down, she'll thank me later. Neko obviously wasn't the one."

"And your showing her that by you getting popped off by him, real forward thinking there Jaz."

"Like I said, it's taken two days to show what time it is."

"With him or you? If your so convinced Neko isn't the one for her, what are you going to do with him? I'm starting to wonder if we're learning more about you than we are about Neko."

"Spare me Tanya, I've been told Chloe how to train Neko ass. He's somewhat of a respectable guy, but not above a little reconditioning."

Tanya and Jazmine continued like this as Chloe got dressed. She was moving mindlessly, intent that she needed to prepare to leave but unsure exactly where she was going. She was well within earshot of the conversation going on in her living room. She actually found truth in what both girls were saying. She saw no need to step in as it seemed both girls were set in their ways. Chloe had learned, and collectively the girls had adopted the rule, "no disputes would be settled by the third." It was too easy and disrespectful to the one of them who suffered simply because their group only included three. She checked herself in mirror as she concluded getting dressed, still aware that she shouldn't look like she was going crazy. Chloe then casually left her bedroom and walked into her living room. She halted the conversation that Tanya and Jazmine thought they were having privately and they watched as Chloe first put on her coat, and then gathered her phone and her keys.

"Chloe, what you doing?"

Tanya said it, Jazmine looked it. She gave a salutatory nod to both and gave instructions to lock up. Then she was gone.

XLIII

Neko could see everything right now. He could see the first time he met Chloe. He could see the first time they made love. He could see the first time he told her he loved her. He could see the time she had been pregnant. This was bad, but he did have a terrible habit of acting really stupid every time Chloe came up pregnant. This was the third time. The first time she had gotten pregnant had only been a few months into their relationship. It had caused quite a strain. Both Neko and Chloe decided to look at it as a sort of trial by fire. They both made promises that they wouldn't make rash decisions without communicating with the other. Neko promised he would give Chloe not only a family and a future, but the world. Then they got stuck. They remained in this space until now. Neko could think of over two or three dozen times he acted out of spite. Countless times, where even though he may have been right, he had taken Chloe for granted. He had taken time for granted. Time with Chloe was something he didn't have anymore. He had risked everything right in the face of them starting a family and for what? A cheap nut with Chloe's best friend? Right now he would do anything to go back to any one argument. Just to stop it right in the middle and let Chloe know that whatever they were arguing about wasn't that important. To just hold her and let her know how important she was to him. Ultimately, to let her know he was done with bullshit, that he was ready to grow up and be a man for her. He probably would never have that chance now. The innocence in their relationship was gone. Too much damage had been done. It was dawning on Neko exactly what he had done. Her best friend was pregnant. Talk show shit. Neko didn't blame her. As he sped to her apartment though, he struggled to remain optimistic. He loved her too damn much not to try. Or if she was completely done, at least to let her know that he was going to accept responsibility for his actions, get out of her way and do whatever was asked of him for the sake of her and the sake of their baby.

Still memories flooded his brain, his eyes reddened as he was overwhelmed by just how many memories they had shared. She was his best friend. He couldn't picture life without her. He grew angry with himself. Why hadn't he thought like this earlier? Why was he only realizing this now that it probably was too late? Neko would probably sell his soul to go back and make sure the two never met at all. Neko was sure she would have ended up with someone with enough sense to take care of home. He'd rather see her happy with somebody else than miserable with him. It amazed him how things he had had major attitudes about just didn't seem that important to him right now. All the times they would argue and he would carry on like a five year old. Chloe would too, but it was pointless. Neko loved her. Right now he carried the burden of knowing his relationship with Chloe had been in his hands and he had fucked it up something royal. The radio blared D'Angelo and Lauryn Hill's "Nothing Even Matters," and Neko couldn't help but feel like somebody, somewhere, was telling him something. He turned into Chloe's apartment complex, where he first spotted Tanya's and then Jazmine's car. That's fine he thought. He didn't know exactly what Jazmine might have told Chloe at this point, but maybe it would be better to clear the air with her as well. As he looked for a park of his own, he almost didn't notice Chloe stride right in front of him. He slammed on his brakes. The two locked eyes. They stayed this way for a moment before Neko motioned Chloe to get in the car. It was clear that Chloe had been crying. There were rings around her eyes that were also a shade of scarlet. Chloe stared at him, then shook her head and continued to her car. Neko immediately put his car in park, jumped out of his car and called out to Chloe, who was unlocking her own car door. She obviously could hear him, but was obviously choosing to ignore him as well.

"Chloe will you at least talk to me? Can I at least explain?"

"Explain what Neko? I've taken sex education before, I'm well aware of where babies come from."

"So that's it then Chloe? We just cease to exist, we split visitation and act like we never happened? I'm sorry for everything that's happened. Most of it is probably my fault. You know what? As a matter of fact, I could care less whose fault it is. I don't have an off switch when it comes to us. I know I screwed up royally, but let's not let it end like this."

"I'm not letting it end like this Neko, you are. But your girl is upstairs; go try your bullshit psychology on her, maybe she'll go. Because if you care anything about me or us, you'll let me get in my car and go."

"Where are you going?"

"Anywhere but here."

"Fine."

As Chloe jumped in her car, Neko got into the passenger side.

"Wherever you go, I go. Remember that?"

"Neko please! Will you stop talking to me like I did this. You forgot! You threw it all away! Stop talking to me like I'm running out on you. You fucked her!"

Chloe was crying now.

"Just go Neko, please."

Chloe looked at him. Neko realized he was doing more harm than good.

"Can we talk at some point?"

"Yes, just not right now."

Chloe was leaning over the steering wheel, sobbing.

"Can I at least drive you where you're going to make sure you're OK?"

"I don't know where I'm going and have you not noticed I'm trying to get away from you and all this. Just let me go Neko."

"I love you Chloe."

Chloe cried out loud, turned to Neko and screamed.

"No you don't! Don't you dare say that! How could you say that after what you've done? Just get out! Go away Neko!"

Chloe's eyes burned. She displayed a look of such hurt and betrayal. Neko felt defeated. He had exercised everything he had. Chloe wanted nothing to do with him at this point. He was actually making things worse.

"You might not believe it right now, but I do love you."

"That's fine Neko, now will you leave?"

And with that Neko exited her car. She immediately pulled off, leaving him standing there.

XLIV

Chloe wrestled with her emotions as she had now left everything behind in theory. She had just left her apartment, with Neko standing dumbfounded outside, while Tanya and Jazmine were probably in similar fashion inside her apartment. She didn't know where she was going and really didn't care. Anywhere was OK to her right now. Usually she would be upset with herself for escaping; Chloe had long bought into the idea that she should have people adjust to her. This was a very simple philosophy that really just broke down to be you at all times. Command your space. If someone enters your space they must adhere to your movements in your space, therefore they must adjust to you. Chloe, a somewhat competitive individual was at present rationalizing to herself how she was still doing that while driving away from her own apartment. She could still see Neko in her rearview as she stopped at the stop sign exiting her apartment complex. His head was down. He had yet to re-enter his truck. She wondered if he would go upstairs and see Jazmine. She wondered what he could have seen in her. Chloe felt small. She had promised herself that if these rumors about Neko and Jazmine were true, that she would not beat herself up about it. More power to them, but it wasn't going that smoothly. She was hurt that Neko had sunk that low. Cheating was cheating, but with her best friend. And Jazmine? Chloe didn't even want to get started on her. Chloe glanced again at her rearview. Neko had looked up noticing she was still there. Like a sad puppy watching his master leave him at a kennel, begging for them to come back but highlighted with sadness that was not universally understood. Serves him well, Chloe thought. She had been trying to speak her disdain for Neko into existence. It was proving to be tough, even though she simmered with anger for him, she still couldn't take her eyes off him. She was having trouble locating the off switch for her feelings.

Chloe hated herself, knowing she would suffer for this soft spot for Neko forever perhaps, especially with the baby in the picture. Right then she decided to stop looking backwards, her mind going with the plan, but her body slower to join in the collective thought.

BAMN!

It happened that fast, with her eyes still fixed on Neko, Chloe had ventured out into the street, only to be met by the force of an oncoming vehicle. The force of the impact knocked her car sideways, activating her airbag as her body was thrown aggressively within the constraints of her safety belt, which luckily she had put on. As her vehicle spun to a stop, Chloe did an inventory. She was still conscious, her leg was stuck but she would be able to move it. She felt a sharp pain in her lower back from the result of being slammed to the side then back.

Neko, who had saw the whole thing, was screaming her name and for someone to call an ambulance. The racket he was stirring up was getting louder. This must mean that he was running towards her. How sweet Chloe thought. At least he's there when she gets "T-Boned" by another car. She was amused at how she could muster sarcasm at a time like this. She looked around to see what she could see. From initial accounts, her car was in bad shape. The other vehicle was not as bad, but Chloe thought for sure her car had taken the worst of the impact. The other driver had exited the car. It looked like some kid. Maybe 17-18 years old. That couldn't be his car he was driving. Chloe wondered if the kid had insurance. She thought maybe not, because he didn't look too thrilled about the damage. Probably wasn't even his car. Chloe wondered what this might do to her insurance premiums. Would they go up? More than likely the guy was asking Neko if he had seen how Chloe had jumped out into the street. Neko was ignoring him as he dialed 911, or at least thats who Chloe assumed he was calling. It seemed as if the kid that hit her was trying to get his story together. When he saw Neko calling whoever he was, the kid immediately went to his glove compartment. No insurance, Chloe thought. She was quite sure she might be in shock for focusing on insurance at a time like this or rather for wondering if she was in shock at all.

She was glad to see Neko ignoring the guy, which to her said at least he was still playing with the home team. He was walking over looking at her; he was speaking to her, asking her if she was OK and if she could hear him. Of course she could, he's screaming. Chloe smiled, thinking to herself that Neko was so very handsome. She wondered why she was letting him get away. Can't win them all she thought. She felt a pain in her midsection. She hoped it wasn't something she ate. She felt like she had to use the bathroom, and actually was doing a self-check to see if she already had. That would be so un-lady like of her she thought. Neko was standing right outside her window now. She thought he was making no sense. Couldn't he see she was OK? She was smiling at him. Handsome devil, Chloe thought. She wondered at that very moment if tomorrow's episode of "The Game" was going to be rerun. Then she wondered why she was thinking about this. Again Chloe wondered if she was going into shock. Finally, she concluded she didn't know, and then maybe she probably was. Then she couldn't remember what was going on. Then she thought she told Neko goodbye. Neko was on his knees now, telling her to hold on. Chloe smiled at him, thinking to herself, "See you later Neko," then everything went dark.

XLV

Neko lay in bed that night, trying to assess all that occurred to him that day. He also wanted to prepare himself for tomorrow, which would be quite a sequel. He'd just arisen off his knees. Neko had been praying. Neko wasn't deeply religious, but he had always been taught that God would listen when nobody else would. Neko was definitely at one of those points where he felt he had no one to turn to. He would probably face ridicule at every corner and every juncture. He wasn't on a quest for sympathy. He was well aware that he had earned his standing, but he knew from his time covering celebrities at work or simply watching TV, that once your business is public knowledge, everyone has an opinion. He was preparing himself for the worst but also asking God for strength. He was aware that he had messed up, but he knew his admission of his mis-steps would have the chance of being looked at as, "just how apologetic is he," or, "did he act sincere?" This was the world he would be entering tomorrow. All this before he and Jazmine's dark secret came to light. Neko was conditioning himself, for he knew whenever that hit the fan, matters and issues would only intensify. He was doing his best to handle one issue at a time but deep down he wanted to grieve for his relationship with Chloe. He was angry at himself that only now he had become quite certain that she was the woman for him. He was quite confident that he was the man for her. He was punishing himself mentally right now for the weird way he'd gone about showing it. As he painted the picture in his head of how this would sound to him if someone confided in him that they were in a relationship where a significant other had slept with a best friend and gotten pregnant, not to mention how everything had come to light,

Neko undoubtedly would have told that person to get as far away from your significant other as possible. But this person was Neko and the significant other was Chloe. He wondered what he would say if Chloe said, OK Neko, why should I give you another chance?" Neko found himself unable to come up with anything that made sense. All he knew is that he loved Chloe very much. Neko also knew that love didn't make sense, but this was pushing it.

Neko questioned what good he had done for Chloe since he had met her. Right now was a shining moment. Chloe lay in the hospital, asleep, after doctors recommended she be kept overnight after being hit by an oncoming car as she was leaving her own apartment. Neko had spent the day trying to explain the events leading up to the accident to policemen, medical workers, insurance agents, and her family. In the morning though, when Chloe would be released, she would be told that she was OK, but that she had lost the baby. Chloe's family had instructed, or rather insisted that Neko not be there. They didn't know the whole story, but they knew something was up between the two. Even Neko had a hard time swallowing the events that had led up to the accident. Ironically, Tanya and Jazmine, dumbfoundedly, nodded in assurance when they were instructed, or rather told to be there. Neko felt compassion for Tanya, contempt for Jazmine, and couldn't even find the words for what he felt for Chloe. This information about her losing the baby would rock Chloe down to her core. This is what she had wanted and probably what had been holding her together throughout all that was going on. But Chloe was going to wake up tomorrow and find out the life inside her was no more. This would happen with Jazmine there, at her family's request.

Neko was basking in Chloe's pain. He wondered if Chloe would play ball and not make a scene, not admit to everyone there that she had been fleeing Neko, not only him but Jazmine as well. Chloe would be well within her rights, but knowing Chloe, she would stomach it all in addition to whatever pain she was in. she would get herself home, insisting to everyone who was worried about her that she was fine. She would do this so they would sleep better. Although the news of what was going on was bound to find the light of day, Chloe would probably take the high road and spare Jazmine and Neko. The police had even gone so far as to question Neko about possibly implicating domestic violence as a reason for Chloe's abrupt attempt to leave her own home so quickly. Neko shot it down immediately; Chloe would no doubt keep it down. Everyone, if it was up to Chloe, would come up unscathed. Only Chloe would carry the pain of what had really happened. Neko felt ashamed, and right then he decided to not let things happen this way. He decided to go to the hospital tomorrow to be with Chloe; even if she didn't want him there because this is what Neko felt like he was supposed to do. Neko continued preparing himself for tomorrow, knowing now that all Chloe would have done without hesitation is what he had to do. Neko would have to operate outside himself for the greater good of everybody else. Neko was starting to buy into the idea that women mature faster than men, because he felt Chloe had been doing this all along.

XLVI

"Ms. Bryant, it looks like you are going to be fine. There were minor back spasms. So I've saw to it you complete a couple of sessions of physical therapy. Unfortunately though, the child you were carrying didn't make it. The trauma from the accident was just too much. We did what we could; you won't be affected with future pregnancies luckily."

The doctor then asked if there were further questions at this time, and let everyone know he would be making rounds for the next few hours but would be available if Chloe had questions. He then exited. Chloe looked around at the faces in the room. She hadn't had a chance to address everyone, but she assumed since everyone now knew that she had lost the baby, that they also now knew she had been pregnant. She scanned the faces in the room, which included her parents, Tanya, Jazmine, and her Aunt Brooklyn, whom she was close to growing up. Everyone expressed insincere well wishes as if they had known she was pregnant, and wished her well for the future. All as if losing a child, at whatever point, was something you just have to get over. They never once showed shock at learning that she had even been pregnant. They prayed for her, and then got her up to speed on her car and the proceedings with the insurance company, who would be furnishing her with a rental.

Jazmine would barely make eye contact, but that was something Chloe could live without anyway. As people spoke, she noticed that everyone was willfully or coincidentally omitting Neko from any and everything of what was going on. He was very much involved as he was the father and had been at the scene of the accident. Furthermore, she knew Neko would have been there. So as everyone pretended he didn't exist, she decided to break the monotony.

"Where's Neko?"

She watched as everyone kind of looked at each other, then to her dad. She assumed from this response or lack thereof, that there had been a combined effort to not bring Neko up.

"Well honey," Chloe's dad Mr. Bryant spoke first, "Neko was very concerned, we've been in contact, but he couldn't make it this morning, he said something had come up."

Mr. Bryant spoke with confidence but still paused at the end as if to see if Chloe would go along with the fictitious account of Neko's whereabouts. Everyone kind of just nodded their heads at the same time, again as if all this had been rehearsed. Chloe nodded, more so because she lacked the strength to go on than because she agreed. She was still heavily sedated and wondered if she was concerning herself with the same things she would be concerning herself with if she was of sound mind and body. There was a silence in the room as if people were unsure who should be talking. Chloe's thoughts were wrapped up in the child lost and Neko. She was set to go home around noon, but found solitude in her thoughts. Why wasn't Neko there? Why was Jazmine there? Why had this happened to her? She began to get upset and she lost her inhibitions.

"So whose idea was it for Neko not to be here?"

This question caused a general expression of "don't look at me" to surface on everyone in the room. Again her father spoke up.

"Baby, like I said, Neko wanted to be here, but he couldn't."

"Bullshit Dad."

Her father looked startled, and shocked at her tone, but more shocked perhaps at the idea she wasn't buying the story. He glanced over at Tanya, who tried to shrug inconspicuously.

"Oh, so you filled him in Tanya?"

Tanya looked guilty at Chloe's insinuation, and shot a look at Chloe's father as if to say "I told you so."

"Chloe, the doctors thought it best if your environment was as stress free as possible."

Chloe shot a nasty look at Jazmine as her father again tried to massage the situation. But no one was paying attention to Mr. Bryant, as everyone saw Chloe's look to Jazmine.

"So this is your idea of stress free," Chloe said with eyes still squarely on Jazmine.

"Chloe, nobody really knows what's going on right now, we tried to do what was best, but its true in doing that, chances were taken."

Chloe had forgotten how good Tanya was at putting things in non-aggressive terms, able to disarm even the most volatile situations. This was probably a walk in the park for her. But Chloe wasn't done.

"Then why is she here?"

Chloe's parent's and her Aunt Brooklyn followed Chloe's eyes to Jazmine, collectively confused. Jazmine squirmed. She was clearly uncomfortable.

"Chloe," Tanya jumped back in, "right now is about the fact that you are OK and to deal with your loss, wouldn't you agree?"

"I agree Tanya. But if that's the case, why is all the politics going on as far as you guys deciding who should and shouldn't be here? Oh, let me guess, it was decided that Jazmine, of all people, should be part of the get well team."

"Chloe these are your friends and you are going to watch your mouth," Chloe's dad shot in.

"Oh you are right Dad. Jazmine is expecting, so we wouldn't want to make her uncomfortable."

Jazmine, at that moment, looked like she would sell her soul to become invisible. She had obviously not expected all this.

"Chloe what has gotten into you?" Chloe's mom finally spoke up.

"Well Mom, it's not so much what has gotten into me as it is what has gotten out of me and into her?"

"Chloe!" Tanya rolled up her sleeves. "What is all this going to change? Is going in on me and the people that care about you going to change anything?"

"Tanya stop talking to me like I instigated all this, where was reasoning when all the bullshit was going on!"

"Chloe!"

Neko entered the room and even Chloe's parents breathed a sigh of relief.

XLVII

Six months later, Neko looked back on the events that unfolded and they still didn't make sense to him. He was quite sure that Chloe still thought about the loss of the child and how much everybody had went through at the time and how it still wore on them. Neko didn't understand how the pain him Chloe shared at the time didn't bring them closer together. Neko figured that Chloe knew as much as he did that there would be tough times, their bond would be reinforced. To Neko, there was just no denying what they had. He wasn't talking about sex or what one or the other stood to gain. But he thought of how close the two had become at that time, how they figured into each other's lives, and how indispensable the two were to one another. Form the unorthodox way the relationship had been forged, Neko didn't see life without Chloe. They had been virtually inseparable since the first week they had started talking. During periods of indecisiveness, anger, and brooding negativity, they endured. It was as if even in the times of turmoil they would rather be angry together, than lonely apart. The magnetism between them grew past lovers and/or friends. Neko often struggled with how he had taken so long to realize what he had. No disrespect to Chloe, she wasn't perfect, but she captured his imagination. He fought this tooth and nail, only to realize now that he had what he wanted not because it felt right to them, but because it felt right to him.

When Neko was a boy, he remembered his mother telling him, "You make people adjust to you." His mother and he didn't share the closest bond, but memories of her growing up were sprinkled with little nuggets like that. These principles, like him, evolved over time, with deeper understanding coming with age. Today, Neko took from this, from his mother's words, how if he loved someone, he should love them not because they deemed it necessary but because he deemed it necessary. He could remember at least a dozen times where he had allowed Chloe to dictate his love output. With all due respect, this was not her power; Neko had given it to her. In no situation does another person deserve to negotiate how you feel. If you love someone, you love them. You give all of yourself and your faith is in the idea that your love will be reciprocated. To Neko, when this situation goes bad, it is similar to the story of the boy who takes his ball and goes home if he's not picked on the team. Or quite simply, this is the behavior of a spoiled brat. Neko knew he couldn't pinpoint particular moments that led to things playing out the way they did, but he always marveled at how sobering time was. How six months later none of the incidentals matter as much, only the love. The theater of the mind that goes on can be cathartic or push you to delirium, he had examined, re-examined, and then again in his mind the "coulda, woulda, and shoulda's." Still there was the love. Love there was no moving on from, just a love that leaves a scar. Sometimes that scar brings terrible memories forth, and at other times it brings a smile as it is evidence that love exists.

Neko daydreamed that at this moment Chloe would have been about seven and a half months into her pregnancy. He chuckled at how her physical appearance would be and just how much more hormonal could she get. Through this Neko was holding on, he hoped his energy was contagious. He hoped, going forward that Chloe would not take the easy route. Even Neko was down on himself and felt he may be bad news. But he believed in him and Chloe and what they could do together. It would be hard. Neko didn't have a plan so to speak, but he thought that a person should always fight for happiness. Most people are content with a feeling of comfort or relief, but true happiness, especially in love, takes faith. Neko wanted desperately to see him and Chloe one day look back on the journey and not feel it's complete. He wanted more, if only to correctly show Chloe that he was capable of loving her. But these were daydreams, back to reality.

XLVIII

"Hmmm.... Well look what the cat dragged in."

Chloe did not allow Neko's entrance into the hospital room to steal her thunder.

"Not right now Chloe. This isn't the time."

"I'm going to need for everybody to stop telling me what I have time for because when I wanted to have time for my child, nobody gave a fuck!"

"Chloe!"

Nobody quite knew what to say to Chloe. Chloe had no idea what to say to Chloe, or to them either for that matter. There was a disconnect in the room. This disconnect was between everybody. Chloe was in such physical and mental pain, furthermore, for the first time being able to face Jazmine and Neko, add the drugs she'd been given, and you have lightning in a bottle. Chloe's parents and her Aunt were finally starting to catch on that it was something going on they didn't quite understand.

Tanya was on the brink of tears, it was apparent that all her time spent in the middle of things was wearing on her. What had made her so effective in this position was her gift of empathy. She sincerely felt what people were going through. But it was so much pain in the room, from everywhere; you could tell she was also beginning to deal with her own as well. It seemed Tanya was deeply troubled and saddened by the carrying on of her loved ones.

Meanwhile, Jazmine too looked like it was just starting to hit her, how heavy gravity can be when pressure is applied against it. She had yet to communicate remorse over what was going on, but it would have taken a figure built of stone to not feel anything for Chloe's disposition at this time.

Then there was Neko. The indifferent antagonist. The key to it all. You could sense his commitment to seeing everything through. His love for Chloe tattooed on his face. His contention to handle his responsibility commendable but fallen well short of what was expected of him and what he expected of himself.

"So what's the doctor say?"

Neko's question was like air being let out of a balloon. Chloe's eyes bugged as if over the past couple of minutes she had been able to outlive the terrible turn of events she was suffering through. She visibly went back to the doctor's grim pseudo-obituary.

"Well Mr. Rose, the baby didn't make it. It's just really unfortunate that I wasn't as smart as you and didn't double up. I guess you are on to the next one."

At this last remark by Chloe, Mr. Bryant had had enough, "Ok, just what the hell is everybody talking about?"

"Well dad, it's really nothing but the circle of life hard at work. As me and Neko mourn our loss, we all can celebrate, as Neko and Jazmine prepare to bring their own little bundle of joy into the world."

What Chloe lacked in candor, she made up for in sarcasm.

"What?"

Mr. Bryant's question was toned perfectly if he was trying to illustrate he didn't quite get what Chloe was getting at, and he didn't.

"Well dad, I was about six weeks pregnant, and believe it or not Jazmine's probably about that as well, and it Neko's. Seems as if lover boy over here was working overtime."

Mr. Bryant got it now, and shot an un-approving stare Neko's way. One of those, "I probably can still whoop your ass" looks. Neko didn't flinch. Either he didn't care or he was prepared for the opinionated onslaught undoubtedly coming his way. It seemed as if Mr. Bryant was going with the former and Neko the latter. That jab by Chloe just about did if for Jazmine, she abruptly left the room. As she exited the doctor entered.

"There's been a mistake, I have wonderful news."

CHLOE: in her own words...

WHAT STARTED FROM A FLICKER SOON BURNED TO A FLAME

WHAT WAS SUPPOSED TO BE FOREVER STARTED WITH A NAME

PUT OPPOSITES TOGETHER PROBABLY COME AWAY WITH GAME

AND TWO BROKEN HEARTS THAT'LL NEVER BE THE SAME

WHERE TO GO FROM HERE CAN BE ANYBODIES GUESS

THE PAIN IS MORE THAN AN EMOTION WHEN YOU FEEL IT IN YOUR FLESH

THOSE THAT SAY IT'LL BE OK PROBABLY NEVER FELT THIS

THAT'S LIKE UNTIL YOU COMMIT SUICIDE YOU HAVE NEVER SLIT A WRIST

SHOULD'VE STOPPED, BUT RIGHT NOW WANNA DO IT AGAIN

LIVING LIFE THROUGH MEMORIES CUZ THERE'S NO FUTURE IN FRIENDS

BUT WHAT DOESN'T KEEP GOING UNFORTUNATELY HAS TO END

WHEN THE LOVE ISN'T STRONG ENOUGH IT HAS NO CHOICE BUT TO BEND

POETIC JUSTICE IN THE MOVIES BUT THIS IS A SLICE OF LIFE

NOT WHAT EVERYBODY SEES NOT TALKING SATURDAY NIGHT

SURE THAT EVERYBODY BELIEVES THAT WHEN THERES A SMILE THINGS ARE FINE

THEY ALSO THOUGHT IT WAS 7:45 BUT IT'S A QUARTER PAST NINE

PUT LIFE ON AUTO KEEP GOING SOMEHOW

CHECK OUT FROM NOVEMBER TO AUTUMN OR TIL THINGS CALM DOWN

TRYNA COPE RIGHT NOW BOUT TO CHOKE RIGHT NOW

COULDN'T BEAR TO SPEAK SO JUST WROTE SOMETHIN' DOWN...